Even now, years *felt the rush of fi* *looking at her.*

His Mei. His wife.

Every cell in his body collided in their haste to get him moving in her direction so he could take her in his arms, but he told himself to wait. To be patient.

He believed with all his soul that there was a solution. There had to be for two people who had loved each other so much.

"Mei," he said. "I want to be your husband again."

She cocked her head, her ponytail shifting off her shoulder. "And I want more than anything to have my husband back. But you made a choice when you left."

"I'm here," he said emphatically. "And I'm going to be here from now on."

Available in June 2009
from Mills & Boon®
Special Edition

The Second-Chance Groom

CRYSTAL GREEN

MILLS & BOON
Pure reading pleasure™

First published in Great Britain 2009
by Harlequin Mills & Boon Limited,
Eton House, 18-24 Paradise Road, Richmond, Surrey TW9 1SR

ISBN: 978 0 263 87047 3

23-0609

Harlequin Mills & Boon policy is to use papers that are
natural, renewable and recyclable products and made from
wood grown in sustainable forests. The logging and
manufacturing processes conform to the legal environmental
regulations of the country of origin.

Printed and bound in Spain
by Litografia Rosés S.A., Barcelona

CRYSTAL GREEN

lives near Las Vegas, Nevada, where she writes for Mills & Boon® Special Edition and Blaze®. She loves to read, overanalyse movies, do yoga and write about her travels and obsessions on her website, www.crystal-green.com. There, you can read about her trips on Route 66, as well as her visits to Japan and Italy.

She'd love to hear from her readers by e-mail through the "Contact Crystal" feature on her webpage!

To Stefania, who's a real-life heroine, and to the
firefighters who also informed me, inspired me
and put their lives on the line every day
to keep us safe.

Chapter One

Five years of marriage, Mei thought as she stood in the open doorway of her apartment, face-to-face with her husband. Five years and it had come to them not knowing where they stood with each other.

Only a millisecond had passed since she'd heard his key in the lock. But it seemed so much longer as she took in every detail of him.

Tall and worked-tanned, with the well-defined muscles of a firefighter who had been honing his body daily ever since he'd decided to dedicate himself to the job. His hair was dark, clipped short, but still long enough to run her hands through. His face was strong-featured, with a chisled jaw and a cleft in his chin. His eyes, a clash of green and gray. His nose, crooked from the time he'd broken it while attempting to administer medical aid to a frantic man his crew had extracted from a burning building.

A hero.

And a husband, too, even though Mei struggled with a terrible fear that battling blazes filled a void that her love couldn't.

"Mei," he said softly.

She was so tempted to run to him….

But *he* was the one who had decided to leave.

Travis turned around to close the door, then gestured toward it.

"I see my key still works…."

"I wasn't sure you'd be here to test it." Her mouth was so parched that the words barely got out. "I told you that if you left this time, you shouldn't come back."

Even though she was trying so hard to stay strong, her skin cried out for one touch, one warm moment of the contact she'd been craving this past month ever since he'd left home.

"And I didn't come back," he said. "At least not when I first returned to Placid Valley a few days ago. But you checked in with my battalion chief, so you'd already know that."

She was glad he realized how concerned she'd been about him while he volunteered to fight a string of brush fires farther south. And she hoped it made him understand just how sick she'd been about leaving things in such an ugly state, after a confrontation that should've happened long before.

But she hadn't truly wanted him to stay away.

Not even if she had given him that last-stand ultimatum borne from all his overtime, extra shifts and nights away from home.

"California Department of Forestry and Fire Protection nearly had those fires contained," Mei said, "but you rushed out there, going from one to the other, as if you were the only force that could stop them."

"Mei—"

"Travis, you know that I *want* you to make a difference. Lord knows I do. But there's an extreme side of you that takes it to the limit, and I'm afraid that side doesn't know when to stop." She fisted her hands, eyes filling with wet heat. "It's as if you can't—or refuse—to see what's been happening to us since—"

"Since…?" he asked. But then he held up a palm, clearly knowing the answer. "Since my mother died in that fire. Since I started crusading because of her death. You don't have to say it."

A haunted cloud filled his gaze, and once again, she didn't know how to chase it away.

"You've done so much good," she said instead, "but what would your mom think of how much time and effort you spend chasing these demons? What would she say if she saw them taking you over?"

A vein stood out in his tensed neck as he held back a response.

She could see he was taking every word to heart, and she only regretted that she'd waited so long to voice what had been coming between them.

"Your mom didn't die because of *you*," she added.

"I know. But her death changed everything—our new marriage, my outlook on life. You signed on for the responsible future CEO you exchanged vows with, not an ultimate firefighter."

True, Mei thought. They'd gotten married at twenty-two. So young. Too naive to realize what was happening while Travis began cutting back to part-time hours in the office and preparing himself, with schooling and volunteering, to earn a place as a firefighter/paramedic with the county.

So young that she had only seen Travis turning tragedy into bravery.

She'd had no idea it would consume him—*them*— especially after Isabel had been born. And that's when Mei had gotten scared.

What if Travis got hurt? What if he…?

She couldn't ever bring herself to think about that.

"I just wish," Mei said, chest tight, "that our daughter and I could see a balance between the fighting and the husband and father we need."

He paused. When he finally spoke, emotion filled his voice.

"Not a day goes by that I don't think of what happened to my mother, Mei. I just want to make sure the same thing won't happen to another son. Another family."

A family like theirs….

She wished this would all go away so she could just close the few steps between them, to hold him. But that wouldn't show him that she took her ultimatum seriously. Giving in would only put them right back where they'd started—with a marriage falling to pieces.

"But," he added, "you already know all that. And I

came back here to strike that balance. I came back to show you that I will do anything to fight for *us*."

Fight. The word conjured a clinging fear that Mei couldn't compete with Travis's demons anymore. That with his mother's death, he had changed and gone down a path leading him away from her and their little daughter.

He took a breath, and she saw the ghosts return to his gaze before she could stop them.

Why *couldn't* she stop them?

He put his keys on the entryway table, and she saw that he still wore his wedding band. She ran her thumb over her own bare ring finger, and that seemed to draw his attention.

But even though his expression grew dark, he didn't point out the painful symbolism.

"Is it Isabel's naptime?" he asked.

"Yes. She's been asking about you."

"And I've been thinking about her…and *you*. During the breaks between each fire, I played and replayed in my mind what you said before I left."

Her ultimatum came back to her loud and clear. "I'm willing to do anything necessary to save us," she'd said. "And unless you feel the same way, there's no use in returning to our home to pretend we're happy with never seeing each other or that *I'm* happy with sitting home and worrying about you beyond your regular shifts. Think about what you're willing to do."

He continued. "You brought up every doubt I'd ever entertained about what was happening between us. Doubts I always tried to excuse as part of my imagination. But that just goes to show how zealous I've been." He met her gaze head-on. "I promised I'd make everything right when I got back…if you'd let me. I love you and our life together, and I'm sorry that ever got away from me."

His confession pierced her. "I love you, too, Travis, but that was never the issue."

Silence tore between them, a wound that cried out to be mended.

Finally, he broke it. "Does Isabel know about…"

"About our separation? No, she doesn't have the first idea."

"Don't—" he made a wiping motion with his hand, as if to shove the word away "—say that."

"What? 'Separation'? Travis, that's what happened. Otherwise, you would've come straight here after you got back into town."

"I stayed at Jed's for a few days." Jed was a buddy from the firehouse. "I was too on edge, tired, from the fires. That wasn't the condition I wanted to be in to talk with you. Then I heard you'd been calling in to check on me."

His gaze told her that this had probably given him enough reason to come through their apartment door again.

Her heart constricted. God, she'd wanted him here so badly, but even now, she kept expecting his phone to ring and he would rush out the door, responding to a summons to come in for more hours, just as he had so many times before.

His gaze hadn't changed from the affectionate tinge it'd taken on when he'd asked about Isabel. "So when's my little girl getting up?"

"Isabel's been down for an hour so far. She played really hard at the beachside park this morning when my mom took her there."

"No preschool today?"

Mei closed her eyes, then opened them. "She goes only three days a week. Which you would remember if you spent more time with her."

As if her comment had wrenched more than emotional space between them, Mei blew out a breath that she found she'd been holding. Her stomach was in knots and she felt dizzy, but that was par for the stressful course lately.

Travis took another step into what used to be their home.

"You seem tired," he said, running a gaze over her.

"Just a little run-down. That's all."

He shook his head. "Dammit, Mei, I'm sorry. This past month took its toll on you…."

"I'm fine."

She flinched at her tone—the anger she'd tried so hard to contain coming through, even if she was so happy to see him again.

At the resulting silence, she fidgeted, anxious. Her gaze flitted from him to somewhere else—anywhere else—then landed on a second entry table, piled with photos she had run through her computer printer.

Chang family pictures from last weekend's extended-clan party. A cousin from Hong Kong, her former home, had been visiting, and Mei had played the part of historian.

Travis glanced at the photos, too, and their eyes locked, making her even dizzier. She wandered away, toward the kitchen counter, then grabbed on to it.

"Guess I missed another gathering," he said.

"They ask about you, my parents. And my brothers and cousins and all the rest."

"What do you tell them?"

What could she say?

I tell them that they shouldn't worry because you're gone so much. I tell them not to lecture me about how they were right about my marrying someone so far removed from my culture and their expectations, someone whom they believed was too hot-blooded to be a good husband in the first place.

Then again, his father was no fan of their relationship, either, and it had even taken his mom a while to come around before she'd passed away.

"The details of our marriage are no one's business but our own," she said.

"Damned straight. Now that I'm not a probie anymore, I even took some more vacation time to come home and see to those details."

"Time off?" she asked, surprised.

But he'd told her he was going to change, right?

He gave a pointed look to her naked ring finger, and neither of them commented further.

Travis walked away, over the hardwood floor, toward the hallway. Somehow, he looked lost amid the bright colors and burbling rock fountains she had positioned out of the reach of Isabel.

Even though the late September afternoon light filtered through the high windows and settled over him, there was still a darkness he hadn't shed.

Mei wondered if he ever would.

And if he would always be fighting it while leaving her and Isabel behind in the process.

"Do you think coming back has really changed anything?" she asked, her throat closing with heat, with an anguish so physical it was taking her over.

"Yes," he said.

He slowly met her gaze, holding it until she couldn't bear to look away.

Then he continued. "Before now, I've gone about everything all wrong, Mei, and from this point on, I'm going to do whatever it takes to make this marriage work."

Across the room, sorrow draped over Mei like a misty veil, making Travis all the more agonized.

Even now, he still felt the rush of first love from just looking at her almond eyes, delicate nose, high cheekbones and full lips. Her fall of black hair, contained in a ponytail, along with her long white T-shirt and jeans, told him that she'd spent most of the day working on her burgeoning Internet baby-clothing line and minding Isabel.

His Mei.

His wife.

Every cell in his body collided in their haste to get him moving in her direction so he could take her in his arms, but he told himself to wait. To be patient. There were still too many hard feelings between them.

His hesitation even went deeper than respecting her feelings. His marriage was in trouble, and he was here to save it.

Just as you try to save everything, said a small voice that he suppressed.

"I realize," he said, "that I can't merely stroll in here and be your husband again, but I'm sure going to try to work up to that."

She stared at him for a long time and he could almost translate her doubts.

Could they save this dying marriage?

Yes. With all his soul, *yes*.

He added, "There has to be hope for two people who love each other so much that they'd withstand the disapproval of their families to be together. We've fought for each other before, and we can do it again."

She cocked her head, her ponytail shifting off her shoulder as she opened her mouth to speak. But a tentative voice calling "Mommy?" broke in.

Mei perked up, turning toward the hallway. "Right here, Izzy."

Travis's chest contracted at the thought of seeing their daughter.

With a glance at Mei—who nodded her head toward Isabel's bedroom, as if telling him to go ahead—he took off down the hall.

Never take them for granted again, he thought, wishing he had realized how necessary it was before Mei had needed to confront him.

Isabel's closed door beckoned with that Pocahontas name sign marking her territory.

That little sign—he'd missed seeing it.

He opened the door, exposing a room busy with dark pink boas hanging from hooks, posters of laughing cartoon characters hanging on the walls and a bed piled high with colorful stuffed animals.

Isabel was sitting between a Bugs Bunny and a Shrek. For a second, she stared at him, blinking, and the irrational notion of her not recognizing him racked Travis. He hesitated.

Her eyes were the light color of his own, but her hair

was as black as her mother's. Her cheeks were chubby and pink, her lips like rosebuds in the few fairy tales he'd read to her.

The last time he'd tucked her in had been more than a month ago.

He came inside, kneeling by the bed.

"Daddy?" Isabel whispered.

"I'm back," he said. "And I've really missed you."

She smiled shyly, and it twisted regret around his heart. Nonetheless, he pulled her into a hug.

So much to make up for….

He breathed in her baby-shampoo smell, his throat constricting as she spoke against his chest.

"I missed you, too, Daddy."

As his daughter clung to him, he saw Mei entering the room out of the corner of his eye. But then Isabel reared back a few inches, inspecting him.

Something welled within his chest—the promise of another chance?

"You coming to my school tonight?" Isabel asked. She had a way of enunciating everything just so.

Mei spoke up. "She has an art show."

Travis tried to act as if he'd penciled this in on his calendar long ago.

"You bet I'll be there," he said, reaching out to touch her tiny shoulder.

In kind, Isabel offered another smile, this one bashfully content. He couldn't help wondering if it was because she was happy that he was able to attend one of her school functions. He'd done so before, but not nearly often enough. Time hadn't allowed it.

Actually, he thought, correcting himself, it was all his crusades that had prevented him from being there.

"I love you, Izzy," he said.

She nodded. "I love you, Daddy."

As a glow settled into Travis, he glanced toward Mei, who had one hand clasped near her heart, as if sheltering it from the damage she expected from him.

He'd inflicted that damage on Mei.

Him—the guy who was so good at stopping destruction in a world outside of his own home.

He hugged his daughter as if to erase all of that. She rested her head on his shoulder.

After a minute, Mei's voice came from the doorway.

"Izzy? Do you want to change into your outfit for tonight?"

"Yes!"

The girl sprang from the mattress and darted to the dressers, where her pink pants and frilly blouse were laid out on the surface.

An adoring smile hovered on Mei's lips as she watched Isabel. When she glanced back at Travis, he was already prepared for the lightning bolt that hit him from the inside out.

Pow.

Mei did it to him every time.

"You sure you don't want to rest?" she asked him. "You've had a long month."

She didn't want him to go, did she? Well, he couldn't blame her, but he was determined to fix everything—and this was step one.

"I'm good. I want to see what kind of masterpieces Isabel's been creating."

Their daughter turned around, already speaking. "Fingerpaints and stuff," she said, hands full of clothing.

Then she donned her outfit, chattering, as if to detract from the words her parents weren't saying to each other. She talked about what she'd done at preschool yesterday, her two friends named Stacy M. and Stacy L., and the playhouse in the school's backyard.

All the while, Travis melded into the flow of simple conversation, liking that he was here to listen to it.

In fact, he was so intent upon Isabel that he was surprised to discover that Mei had left her post at the door.

Dressed now, their daughter glanced at the spot where her mother had formerly waited, then did this odd shrugging motion that Travis had never seen before.

But before he could comment, she sniffed at the air, which carried the aroma of marinara sauce.

"Dinnertime!" she said, then ran toward the kitchen, leaving Travis in her dust.

After he followed her there, he found that Mei had left them alone to fix a quick dinner of rotini pasta, salad, orange slices and bread.

Or had it just been too hard for her to watch him with Isabel, all the while knowing that he might be out the door the next minute?

With the food on the table, Isabel asked questions about the brush fires—"They were long ones this time," she commented—and Travis answered every query, downplaying the danger as he sensed how Mei's eyes had taken on that wary look that most all the wives tried so hard to contain.

Travis ended the subject, concentrating on dinner instead.

When the meal ended, they all went down to the parking garage where Mei's silver, family-friendly Galaxy was parked alongside Travis's red pickup.

While Mei packed the back with her purse and various bags, Travis secured Isabel into her car seat, even though she insisted she could do it herself. Still, he checked that the straps held.

After shutting Isabel's door, he passed Mei on her way to the passenger seat.

"You don't want to drive?" he asked, wondering if taking the wheel would be akin to taking over when Mei had spent so much time watching over Isabel while he was gone. He didn't want to shove his way into their routines, and that unsettled him, emphasizing again how he wasn't even a part of their week.

"No," she said, presenting the keys. "I'm always one to grab an opportunity to be chauffered around town."

He raised an eyebrow, then accepted the keys, their fingers brushing.

Electricity—pent-up desire—jarred him, and she gasped, her gaze going hazy.

But then, as if remembering that he might fall back into old habits any second now, she went to her seat and softly closed the door.

Travis stood at the rear of the car for a moment longer, his skin recovering from the contact, his body and soul burning for the wife he hadn't seen—or touched—for nearly a month. But he was going to do everything in his power to be a true husband again.

Everything.

Chapter Two

"It's so wonderful to finally meet you," said Mrs. Willens, Isabel's blond and bubbly preschool teacher.

As she held out a welcoming hand to Travis at the classroom doorway, Mei couldn't help but notice the ruddiness his skin had taken on at Mrs. Willens's innocent comment.

Embarrassment because this was the first time he had made it to his daughter's school this year?

She wished she could tell him it was okay, that she and Isabel were so happy to have him here with them, but the words didn't come very easily—not in a crowded gathering with a group of other mothers waving at her from across the room and Isabel already running around the minitables and chairs with her friends.

"It's great to meet you, too," Travis said, shaking the teacher's hand in return, his smile the sign of a man trying his best. "I know Isabel really enjoys you and the activities you dream up for her, and I'm glad I get to see both, even if I haven't made it here before now."

"The school year started only a few weeks ago," she answered, turning her bright smile to Mei, including her in the conversation, "and I'm just getting to know most of the parents." Back to Travis. "But Isabel and Mei talk about you in such a way that I feel as if I'm meeting a rock star."

He glanced at Mei, as if mildly surprised she boasted about him to everyone. It ached to suspect that her ultimatum might have made him think that she didn't value his hard, heartfelt work, in spite of everything else.

It disturbed her that he didn't know how much she admired him, that he only recognized her frustrations.

"Travis is just back from those brush fires." Mei hoped he would hear the pride in her tone.

And maybe he did, because his gaze lingered on her. She touched his dark T-shirt near his side, a tacit way of telling him that even though they had ridden over in the car with so much strain and silence between them, she really did want to make their way through it.

"Then welcome back, Mr. Webb," the teacher said. "And thank you for doing what you do. There would've been a lot more deaths and lost homes if those fires had gotten out of control."

Travis shrugged, but Mei knew he was pleased, and in some strange way, that made her glow, too.

Before she could even think of how to tell him a fraction of what was in her heart, he said, "The winds finally died down and that eventually made our jobs easier."

Her next words tumbled out in a soft-spoken rush. "It wasn't the winds as much as men and women like you."

Travis glanced at her once more. Their love, which had never disappeared, beat between them.

But Mrs. Willens was already talking and motioning around the room, where rainbow-hued paintings, drawings and murals were displayed under the warming lights.

"We're glad you're back in time to see what your daughter has done," she said, effectively stamping out the emotion-taut moment and claiming their attention again. "Isabel has brought in a lot of her work from home, where I hear she spends most of her time looking at how-to drawing books and creating things like monsters and skeletons. Halloween's more than a month away, but she's already in the spirit."

"It's her favorite holiday and she's seen the premature store displays," Mei said, still vibrating from that shared glance with Travis. "Even more so than Christmas. We've already started putting together about three costumes."

Travis spoke up. "She likes all that dressing up."

He'd said it as if wanting to show that he knew something about Isabel, too, and Mei smiled encouragingly at him. But she could tell he was uncomfortable being here, pretending that they were a whole family.

Another couple and their son arrived, and Mrs. Willens waved them into the room.

"Have a look around," she said, "and in an hour, we'll be having a short sing-along before the festivities end. The students love that part."

They thanked her while she headed for the doorway, leaving them alone.

Standing there, looking like a couple amid all the laughing and contained chaos of the classroom, Mei didn't know how to act. As if they didn't have a care in the world?

Ironically, Travis's voice soothed her out of the anxiety.

"What do you think Isabel will be?" he asked. "For Halloween, I mean."

"Well," she said, turning to face him, her body rattling with suppressed emotion. "There's a fairy princess, or a Care Bear, or maybe even Robin."

"Batman's Robin?"

Mei laughed, and it was the first natural thing she had done all day. "Yes, believe it or not. One of the boys here always pretends to be Batman, and I think she's got a little crush. Robin is her way of impressing him."

"A boy, huh?" He glanced around the room. "Where is this kid?"

Again, Mei found a laugh escaping from her chest, and Travis raised an eyebrow at her, his smile tilted.

Just like old times, she thought, giving in to the fantasy.

A female voice broke in to the thought. "Couldn't resist a good party, either?"

It was Geena, a single mother Mei often chatted with when picking up Isabel from school. Although Mei never revealed anything deep about herself and Travis, she knew all of Geena's story: divorced for two years, engaged now. She seemed much younger than Mei, always wearing her auburn hair in braids and chatting about the latest band she had seen playing in San Francisco clubs.

Next to Geena, a conservatively coiffed man hung back in his business suit.

"I don't know about you two," Mei said, "but I came

for the sugar cookies." She rested her hand on Travis's arm. "This is my husband, Travis."

As the word *husband* rang in the aftermath, Travis greeted the other woman, and Geena introduced her fiancé, Jason, in return.

"When's the big day?" Travis asked.

"December fourteenth." Geena showed off her diamond ring. "Radiohead is going to be in town that night, and that's how we're going to start off our honeymoon—with our favorite group. We met at their concert."

Mei and Travis nodded, and she wondered if Geena's ensuing pause meant that it was time for her to present their own love-at-first sight story.

Worst timing ever.

Luckily, two other couples joined them, but Mei could sense Geena checking Travis out and probably even wondering why there was an invisible canyon between Mei and the man she had always loved…and felt she had lost.

But couldn't tonight be an improvement beyond that?

As they chatted about their children and then the upcoming sing-along—which Geena's fiancé in particular was dreading—Mei glanced down to find Isabel standing near Travis's leg and looking back and forth between her parents.

Mei's heart cracked when she noticed the confusion in their daughter's eyes, as if Isabel had picked up on the obvious tension.

And when she made a nervous shrugging motion—a habit that had become apparent lately—Mei crumbled all that much more.

Just when she was about to bend down to Isabel so she

could gather her into her arms and tell her everything would be all right, that there was no need to think something was wrong with her parents—even if it were a lie—their daughter tugged on Travis's jeans.

"Daddy?" she whispered while the other adults continued to talk.

He lowered to one knee, holding Isabel's hand, and the sight went a little way in quelling Mei's fears.

"Hey, Izzy," he said softly. "You having fun?"

She nodded, then pointed toward an art wall, this one featuring drawings. "Want me to show you my pictures, just like I showed Mommy yesterday?"

"You bet."

Travis stood, turning to the adults, eyes bright. "Don't mind me and Isabel doing some art gazing."

Everyone told him to live it up while Mei fought the temptation to go with them, to be with her family and not anyone else.

But Isabel dashed ahead of her dad, clearly excited to be with him again.

At the same time, Travis's walk was looser than before, and Mei wondered if, in addition to being thrilled about Isabel's invitation, he was relieved at the break from having to act like a happy couple.

More than ever, she realized how far they had to go, even if he *had* come back home.

They got back to the apartment just after prime-time TV started.

Travis knew the show schedules because, in the firehouse, filling the hours until a call summoned the crew was par for the course, and often he and the guys marked the hours by seeing what was on the tube.

But here, the lack of noise and action set him on edge as they passed the family room's blank TV while he and Mei took a sleeping Isabel to her bed.

What was his problem? Did he need to be back in action *that* badly?

Travis suspected the answer, and he didn't like that every one of his instincts screamed for him to be ready for a call. Didn't like that he had to get back at the thing that had not only put his marriage in danger but had robbed him of a mother who had come around to finally accepting Mei. A mom who had been trying to persuade Travis's father to do the same.

Putting that all behind him, he laid his daughter down on her bed, pausing to brush a finger over her cheek.

Mei watched from the doorway. But as Travis left the room, she came inside to press a kiss to Isabel's forehead and adjust the covers around the child's neck.

The sight pinched. It was as if he and Mei had staged their big ultimatum blowout only an hour ago, the words still crackling between them. Nothing had been resolved yet. How could it be when the ultimatum had only been a symptom of much bigger issues?

Shutting the door behind her, Mei entered the hallway. They walked toward the family room.

"Well," he said, "that show seemed to go just fine."

"The art show?" Mei asked.

Travis gestured toward their daughter's room. "No, our show. We actually seemed like a reconciled couple these past few hours."

"Isabel is sensitive to what's going on, even if we managed to fool everyone else."

Her tone was tired, and he hated that he made her so exhausted.

He stopped walking, and she did, too. They were at the edge of the family room, where a rock fountain burbled in taunting serenity.

"I've noticed this little shrug thing she does," Mei said, providing an example by cricking her neck and raising her shoulders. "It's been happening more frequently."

"I noticed, too. No doubt she does that because she's stressed out about us."

"Children see a lot. Even what we've tried so hard to ignore."

God, just another piece of damage he'd wrought.

He clenched his jaw.

"Travis," she said, responding to his self-disgust by almost touching his arm, then drawing back as if recalling what they'd said to each other before he'd left a month ago.

It killed him that he was so close to her, yet so unable to reach out and stroke her arm, her face. Just the longing for some contact sent a splitting current all the way up his arms.

She seemed to recognize his yearning—a spark that had never died. He could tell he'd affected her because her eyes had gone wide.

As if chasing off goose bumps, she rubbed her arms. "Maybe we should talk this out tomorrow, while Isabel's at school and after you've gone back to Jed's for some sleep."

"Probably not a bad idea. I don't want Izzy to have any more reason to worry."

"Okay." She stood there, as if wanting to say something more, but then she sighed. "Next time she has a checkup, I'll ask the doctor for advice. Meanwhile, there's always the Internet. I'll look up suggestions there, too."

"I'm the one on vacation. I can take care of all that."

Her gaze went soft, as if the shield of that ultimatum had been lifted so the woman who used to trust him implicitly could peek out.

Then she surprised him by heading back into the hallway, toward the linen closet to extract a set of blue sheets, then a comforter and pillow.

"On second thought," Mei said, coming back with the bundle, "Isabel's going to stress even more if she realizes that Daddy isn't even sleeping at home."

"Right." He took everything as she handed it over. So he wouldn't be sleeping in the same bed with his wife, but he was counting his lucky stars he'd even gotten this far. "I'll take care to be up and about before she sees I'm camping out, though."

"Good idea."

He followed her to the guest room, a pale-mint area that wasn't so much decorated with sparse furnishings as stripped of them. Mei put the sheets down the on the bare mattress and began to transfer several piles of the baby clothing she designed to the floor.

They rarely had guests, so she had rejected frilly decoration in favor of workroom function since this was where her growing Internet business, Baby Boom-Boom, was housed. Her computer system rested on an old table in one corner, while in another, a sewing machine reigned. Near the walls, packing boxes waited to be filled and shipped.

She'd wanted to create the business after becoming a stay-at-home mom, and they'd used dividends from Travis's family business stocks as start-up money, seeing as he was already pursuing a paramedic job by then, as a stepping-stone into the fire department.

Come to think of it, Baby Boom-Boom had been the first sign of Mei going her way and Travis going his, and he'd never even known it.

Maybe Mei hadn't, either.

He stepped forward to help her put the sheets on the bed. The sight underlined their separation. The linen would smell of her, because laundry detergent and dryer sheets were a part of Mei's daily perfume. A wife, a homemaker, a mother. She was everything.

When they were done, she smoothed out the comforter.

"Time to hit the sack, then," he said. "I can see how tired you are, and I'm ready myself."

She paused, as if still deciding something.

Was she reconsidering having him in the apartment?

Or… No, he wouldn't even hope that she was thinking of bringing him into their bedroom.

She confirmed that when she turned to leave, and his stomach sank.

But, before she closed the door, she said, "We need a night to think a little more, before we get into the big talk. At least, I do."

"Absolutely," he said, fluffing a pillow.

"Travis?"

He glanced her way, finding her leaning against the door frame, pink circles under her eyes. It slayed him to see her in such beaten shape.

"I'm still not over it," she said softly. "Any of it. So the last thing we probably need is to gloss over things by pretending to roll merrily along. I'm glad you seem to understand that."

He felt as if he'd been pummeled. And deservedly.

She gauged him for a little, then came closer, yet still kept a distance.

He shivered at her proximity, trying to shut out thoughts of how she felt, smelled, tasted. The only sounds he could hear were his thudding pulse, his strained breathing. God, he wanted her back.

He caught the rhythm of her own breathing, and he closed his eyes, imagining another night, another time, when he could've so easily reached out to hold her against him, to kiss her until his body cried for more....

He shifted, but only because he wanted to get nearer to her.

Just an agonizing inch. Just a whisper.

But then, as if knowing this wasn't yesterday—a time when turning to each other would've held no consequences—she turned and left.

Causing his conscience to pain him even more.

The next day started early for Mei. Heck, it wasn't as if she'd been able to sleep with Travis down the hall, anyway. Besides, she couldn't stop imagining him waking up next to her, watching her as the sun rose through the window, his hand reaching out to caress her fully awake....

But she couldn't stand torturing herself like that, so she showered before Isabel got up, then pieced herself together for the coming day.

She needed to prepare for Travis.

Her stomach churned, so she sat down for a moment on the bathroom's tiled floor. Before he'd left, she'd been on the tail end of bronchitis until it had cleared out with the use of antibiotics. However, sometimes she wondered if she'd completely gotten over the illness with this stress. Her body hadn't been functioning normally at all, in fact, but she chalked it up to the circumstances.

The circumstances…

Before she could stop it, anger threatened, but Mei beat it back. She wasn't that kind of person, didn't want to live with the discomfort of knowing she could lose her control at any time….

She talked herself into a calm groove, then emerged from her bedroom, seeing that Travis was already awake, too. In fact, he was cooking pancakes with whipped-cream smiles and strawberry eyes, which had evidently drawn Isabel out of bed extra early, as well.

After everyone said their good mornings—politely, of course, but hardly with any carefree confidence—Mei sensed that their daughter's affection for Travis was still halting, as if Isabel were waiting to see how long her father would be around this time.

Mei dreaded the day the little girl would realize that her daddy's heart was divided, so she went to the table, where Isabel was eating her breakfast, and gave her an all-consuming hug.

In return, Isabel kissed Mei, leaving a sticky-syrup mark on her cheek.

After breakfast, Travis told Mei that he would take their child, who had donned her tiny plastic firefighter helmet, to school today. Mei accepted gratefully. He'd also told her that he would go grocery shopping, then run a couple of errands before returning.

In addition to everything else, his willingness to play household helper would allow her to get an early start on packaging some clothing that needed to be mailed for Baby Boom-Boom. Mei was even sending a receiving blanket and various onesies out to her new friend, Naomi, who hadn't spent long in Placid Valley before she'd fallen in love then moved away to New York, where the pregnant woman had just gotten married.

But before Mei whisked off that particular package, she intended to run down to the nearby Suds Club Laundromat and have Naomi's friends sign a congratulations card before Travis got back.

Besides, Mei could use the comfort of her pals before she and Travis got down to the nitty-gritty. Truth was, her friends at the Suds Club had been a saving grace lately; they were like an extended family in many ways, bolstering her during this rough time.

So when she walked the short distance from the apartment to the Laundromat, she was ready to catch a few minutes of her favorite soap opera, *Flamingo Beach,* which everyone who came to the Suds Club at this hour was there to enjoy.

She entered, the bell on the glass door dinging, the detergent smell enveloping her. Across the room, a TV was bolted in a corner of the ceiling, playing preshow commercials and competing with the bustle of clothes in washers and dryers. Below the screen, a group of club members were toasting one another with sodas from one of the machines.

"Evina, Evina…!" they were all chanting, laughing as they hugged an East Indian club member dressed in a sheer red wrap over her long printed skirts.

The woman danced along with their rhythm, raising her arms above her head in some kind of victory. Mei's heart gave a leap as she headed over. Looked like a celebration.

One of the women spied Mei and spread her arms out in greeting as she intercepted her. Jenny Hunter, with her Marilyn Monroe hair and breezy sophisticate stroll, was dressed in casual yet crisp white pants and a silky shirt that she had tied at the waist. On Wednesdays, she worked from home instead of her office, and this was her lunch hour.

"Evina did it!" the blonde said. "She sold her first freelance story to *America's Woman* magazine."

Instinctively, Mei linked arms with Jenny so she could go over to the joyful group and congratulate Evina.

The lauded author thanked Mei, never knowing that her success wasn't quite enough to chase away Mei's own issues for the day.

But nothing got past Jenny.

Afterward, the businesswoman walked Mei over to the snack machine, where she bought a bag of salted peanuts.

"You're looking more thoughtful than ever," Jenny said, opening her package, then offering Mei a handful of nuts.

Mei took a couple. "Travis came home last night."

The other woman lifted her eyebrows. "And…?"

Mei gave her friend a condensed version of events. She'd been thinking over every detail since he'd returned, and she was tired of getting nowhere with her emotions… and conclusions.

"Seeing him was like…" Mei waved her hands around.

"Like New Year's fireworks?"

One of Mei's hands came to rest over her heart, which was blasting. Thinking about seeing him wound her up, but it ran her down, too.

"Like fireworks," Mei repeated. "And I don't want that because they cloud everything else in the end. I'm so afraid that passion is the only thing that's been keeping us together, besides Isabel. It can't possibly fix anything."

Jenny held a nut between her fingers, considering. "Then again, you said he's willing to listen to you."

"Sure, but what if his inner drive is so strong that I don't have a chance to overcome it?"

"What if you're 'what if-ing' the situation into hopelessness?" The other woman rubbed Mei's arm. "I've seen how down you've been these past few months, but now's your chance to fix that, Mei. Travis sounds all too willing."

"Yes, he does, doesn't he?" Mei said. "You don't think my ultimatum guilted him into—"

Jenny interrupted. "Whoa, whoa, whoa, now. Where's the fearless Internet businesswoman I know?"

Mei smiled. "Right here?"

"Exactly. She's right here."

The other woman led Mei toward the TV seats, where the commercials were almost over.

But as they passed a row of dryers, a voice in a corner caught their attention.

"Want a piece of advice?"

Mei and Jenny turned to Liam McCree, the resident male who pretended that he didn't watch *Flamingo Beach*. As always, he was working on a laptop computer designing some Web site while wearing slacker garb: an open long-sleeved button-down over a T, tattered jeans and hiking boots. Actually, he reminded Mei of an intriguing gypsy, with his dark brown hair and slight goatee.

Jenny took up her normal chin-tilted posture when it came to addressing McCree. "Advice? What, are you suddenly a fortune-teller?"

Sparring was a common event when it came to McCree and Jenny. Hence, McCree merely shrugged.

"I can be pretty handy to have around."

Jenny tugged Mei toward the soap opera, muttering something under her breath about "too much information."

They got to their seats and the introductory scenes for *Flamingo Beach* came on.

Jenny leaned over and patted Mei's hand. "We'll work this out," she said. "We girls always do."

As her friends sat around Mei, smiling, laughing, she took strength from them, thankful to have such a support team.

Feeling better, Mei exhaled, more prepared than before to go to war for her marriage.

Chapter Three

When Mei got back to the apartment, she found that her husband had gotten home earlier than she'd anticipated.

His hair sleep-ruffled, he was wearing one of his dark, cheeky T-shirts, this one with a cartoon R2-D2 beeping at Princess Leia. Mei almost laughed when she saw that the beeps were translated in parentheses as "Nice buns!"

Travis and his T's. The thing was, Mei realized that she had just washed that shirt. She often slept in them when he was gone, just to feel close to him.

Then she realized he was in the kitchen because he was rearranging the cupboards.

She surveyed all the canned goods stacked on the stainless steel counters, all the pots and pans hanging over the center island in new order.

"Hey," he said. "My trip to the stores didn't take long,

so I grabbed a nap to catch up on sleep. When that didn't go too well, I thought I'd make myself useful."

"Thank you. But I wish you'd get more rest, too."

"Yeah, but you know me—never able to settle down." He opened a tall cupboard to reveal an entire network of new storage racks. "I came up with a system. Figured some spring cleaning or autumn cleaning—might save you effort in the long run. And I'll be cooking more, so it's a plus for me, too."

Her heart warmed, but it broke a little, also, when she remembered some of the things they'd said to each other before he'd left.

His phone rang, vibrating on the counter, and his hand darted out for it. His excitement hadn't abated from every other time he'd jumped at an extra-hours overtime call.

But now he jerked his hand to a halt.

Both of them looked at each other.

Instead, he set about arranging dishes in a cupboard above him. A muscle bunched near his jaw.

With trepidation, she checked the caller ID.

"It's Jed," she said.

"He'll leave a message."

Travis continued his task, just as if the ultimate solution was that easy. But his motions were too deliberate, and she realized he really did know that nothing was as simple as it seemed when a couple first fell in love.

She cleared her throat, setting her small purse and his phone on the counter. Her stomach tumbled, but it was because of nerves this time.

He peered at the flower-patterned plate in his grip, then carefully set it back down. Bracing his hands on the counter, he canted toward her. So tall, so imposing, so lethally gorgeous that she couldn't think straight.

But she collected herself, even though her pulse banged in her head, her chest, and then lower....

"Just so you know," he said, "when my vacation time is up in a week, I'm cutting back on the hours."

Relief filled her. "That's great."

"And," he added, "I'm going to look into a transfer to Station Two."

His knuckles had turned white while he gripped the counter, and Mei could tell the mere idea of a transfer was eating at him.

"Isn't Station Two much smaller?" she asked. "A three-man-crew shift? You work at a bigger station with more hustle and bustle near the city, and..."

"What?"

Here it went. "You've mentioned before that only a fraction of the calls at Station Two are fire-related— mostly false and medical. They don't even get out the door half as much."

"That's the idea."

"It's a *wonderful* idea." She steeled herself. "I'm only wondering if you'll end up hating it."

"And if I'll start to resent you and Isabel for taking me out of the action."

He grabbed another plate, put it in the cupboard, and she knew that he was warding off the eventual possibility of her comment.

He was trying so hard.

Still, she could just hear her parents now. *Didn't we tell you he would prove us right? From the beginning, we saw that he was too rash, too impulsive. He turned from his father's wishes and married you, Mei. If only he'd listened, because he is unstable, and he influenced you to go against us, as well.*

They'd been overreacting, but she'd known what they also meant, what went unsaid. They'd wanted her to settle down with a responsible, dependable man of her own background who fit all their expectations, and she had disappointed them. Their disapproval needled her, because they'd been her pillars when she was thirteen and her family had come over to the U.S. from Hong Kong. And they had supported her while she struggled to fit in here in America, to succeed, to be proud of her accomplishments and to grasp every dream.

She didn't want to see the looks on her parents' faces if they knew they had been right all along. She couldn't stand the thought of it.

Almost desperately, she folded a hand over Travis' wrist, holding on and preventing him from continuing his diverting task.

"I'm really glad you didn't say you were going back to your family's corporation," she said. "That would've been the very opposite extreme."

He ran a thumb over the bottom of her arm, the soft side, causing shivers to ruffle her.

"Sitting at a desk and being primed to take over the business one day?" he asked. "Worthless, especially when I could be out there."

His gaze burned, chilling her because the demons hadn't gone away at all.

"I just want you to be happy," she said. "*Us* to be

happy. We're striving for that balance between work and home, remember?"

"*You're* what I want."

He said it with such passion that she couldn't breathe for a moment.

She held him all the tighter, only wishing she were enough to chase all the ghosts in his eyes away.

Time brought them to the point where Mei had to pick up Isabel from preschool after running a few errands for her business, so they'd agreed to meet for a casual dinner at the mall's food court in a couple of hours.

After installing more new organizer trays in the kitchen cupboards and calling it a day, Travis headed for the meeting spot, getting there first and claiming a table. And when he spied Mei and Isabel weaving their way through all the people carrying orange-colored trays, he got to his feet, feeling as if the sun had risen inside of him, lifting him up.

His family.

But a darkness still shrouded him, turning and revolving over his mind's eye, blocking Mei and Isabel's approach like an eclipse.

His mom, trapped in the flaming building. A hand, reaching out to be saved and him not quite grasping it…

As Travis shoved the terrible fantasy away, he realized that he was fisting his own hand. Slowly, he relaxed it, focusing instead on his wife, his daughter.

Across the food court, Isabel gave a little wave to him while holding Mei's hand.

It was as if his daughter hadn't really been expecting

him to be here, after all. But she looked happy that he was, and his heart swelled all the more.

At the last moment, she broke away from Mei and sprinted toward him, and he bent down to her height, grasping her hands. Then, when she fell against him for a hug, he held on for dear life.

"There's my girl," he said, throat tight. "How was school?"

"Good." She backed away to face him. "We played puppets today. And we dressed up and I was a bumblebee. And we listened to stories about princesses."

"You did?"

"Yes, but I ate lots of candy Stacy L. gave to me and Mommy said that made me hyper."

She parsed out her words, as if still having to think a little every time she created a sentence. She'd been less fluent a month ago, it seemed.

Amazing how much a child could change in that short of a time....

By this point, Mei had arrived. She gently tugged on one of their daughter's pigtails. "That's right. When you have too many treats, the sugar winds you up so that you have trouble settling down. Like now."

Travis caught Mei's half-amused tone and held on to it because there was such affection in her voice.

"Well, Izzy," he said. "I expect you'll be working off that energy now?"

He glanced at the artfully arranged jungle gym near their table.

Isabel jumped and clapped. "Watch me, Daddy. I can do tricks."

Travis grinned, then tracked her energetic progress to the amusement area. It pinched at him to see her trying so hard to win his full affections now that he was back. Yet he was going to give her all the time in the world to show both her and Mei how important they were to him.

He laughed as Isabel waved once again, then he turned to Mei.

There was a glint of longing in her eyes that was so fierce it contracted his chest.

She hitched in a breath, and he saw the effect he had on her, too.

As if mutually affected, they turned their attention to Isabel as she showed off by swinging from a low blue bar, then switching to a green one.

Moved by this moment—of feeling as if he belonged again—he started to reach across the table to put his hand over hers, then thought better of it. Even though she'd made the first move and touched him back at the apartment, there was still a cautious vibe between them, as if she thought he would jerk every new promise right out from under her.

The thing was, he *wanted* to move to Station Two, a place where they played lots of pool and had all the time in the world to polish the engine.

Still, he shifted in his seat. Even the thought made him agitated.

But why?

Isabel had trotted back to them, and her voice lifted him back to where his mind should be.

"My tummy's hungry!" she said.

Travis sent Mei a knowing smile, and she lifted her hands in an accepting "Isabel's tummy is often hungry" gesture.

"What's your stomach yelling for tonight?" he asked their daughter, seizing this lighter moment.

She didn't understand, so he asked straight out what she wanted to eat. Sometimes she seemed so precocious that he forgot that she was still learning her way around communicating on a more mature level.

Then he went to get their food while Mei took out some antibacterial gel and doused Isabel's hands with it.

When he returned, she squeezed some liquid onto his hands, too, then rubbed the gel into his skin. Although her touch was innocent, it was all too sensual for Travis.

A month, he thought while her skin lit friction against his, making his belly fist in anguished need. *How did I go a whole month without her?*

When Mei finished, her hands lingered.

So warm.

He couldn't help remembering what the rest of her would feel like against him….

"Guess what?" Isabel said, totally unaware of the way her parents had come to lock gazes.

Mei slowly blinked, then backed away from Travis, clearly recalling that she'd been brought to the point of having to give him an ultimatum not too long ago.

When she disconnected, it felt as if the earth had dropped out from under his feet.

Conjuring a smile, Mei focused on their daughter. "And what are we supposed to guess, Izzy?"

Travis almost could've sworn that they hadn't just had a moment at all.

Except for the tingle of his hands.

And the erratic thud of his heartbeat.

Isabel fidgeted in front of Mei. "I learned a new dance. Want to see it?"

"Most definitely." She sat down, lavishing Isabel with her full attention.

Travis followed her example, even though his skin still flared, alive. Needful.

Isabel offered them both a shy smile when Travis grinned at her in encouragement.

"What's this dance called?" he asked.

"The Captain Underpants," she said.

Captain...what?

Oh, yeah. Now that Travis thought about it, he remembered reading some of those books to her and had seen her play those animated Captain Underpants games on the computer. He was surprised, because he'd thought the cartoon superhero was more of a boy thing. Then again, they hadn't forced dolls on their daughter; Mei and Travis had agreed that Isabel would discover likes and dislikes on her own. All the same, their daughter *had* gravitated toward dolls.

Isabel beamed. "I don't have a cape."

"Excuses, excuses," Mei said.

At that, Isabel hid her body from casual observers between two large cement plant pots, then commenced a strange yet adorable dance. She pulled her arms back and threw her hips forward, then repeated the move again and again. Every few seconds, she'd wink.

Travis and Mei cracked up, and that seemed to egg their daughter on until she zipped back to her seat. Once there, she laughed with them, as if half embarrassed and half ecstatic that she'd entertained so thoroughly.

Although the moment didn't exactly break all the ice, it did offer a sliver of connection between Travis and Mei. A sharp awareness through laughter.

Through…possibility?

From that point on, Isabel asked Mei and Travis to tell her about Disneyland rides. To her, the stories were like adventurous tales, so they obliged, taking turns so Travis could wolf down his shrimp tacos and Mei could finish up her salad.

By the end of their meal, it seemed as if the momentum was definitely going their way.

Until Isabel saw a young couple coming to sit a few tables away, an infant waving its arms from the confines of its carriage.

"Baby!" their daughter said excitedly.

Mei busied herself by cleaning up their trash. "You looked like that once, Izzy."

Travis took Mei's load from her, their hands brushing just as they had last night. Desire zinged through his fingers, up his arms, all over his body. He saw the same response in the parting of Mei's lips, the flare of her eyes.

Then their daughter said, "I want a baby."

That was enough to yank Travis out of the moment.

"I mean," Isabel said, "I want a *baby*. A…"

She searched for a word, but Mei obviously knew what their daughter was talking about.

"A brother or sister," she said softly.

"Yes!" Isabel clapped, eager for their answer.

But Travis still couldn't respond.

And it saddened him to see that Mei couldn't, either.

* * *

Isabel's baby question seemed to permeate the car's atmosphere on the way back home.

It soaked into the closed-in brass elevator, too, as well as the apartment's wider spaces.

And when eight o'clock rolled around and Isabel went to bed, the tension that the query had created only seemed to multiply.

After tucking their daughter in, Mei walked by Travis's side down the hallway. They were heading toward the family room, where the TV provided neutral white noise. She'd come to like the comfort of the sounds while Travis was on shift, so she normally turned it on at night, just as she'd done out of habit when they'd walked into the apartment.

Still, Travis muted it when they sat down—he on the blue-upholstered couch and she across from him on a matching ottoman. On the television, a lioness prowled over a savannah, compliments of the Discovery Channel.

"Leave it to a babe in the woods to stir up trouble," Travis said, tossing the remote aside and leaning back.

"Isabel's baby question didn't make you wonder?" Mei asked.

"If we're ever going to have sex again?" Travis grinned, sliding his hands behind his head.

Cheeky man. "If we'll get to the point where we'll have more children."

His gaze burned into hers, and the oxygen left her lungs. She struggled to get it back.

What could they say now?

God, she knew what the deepest, most primal part of her wanted to say, but her protective senses silenced it.

I want you so badly it hurts, she thought. *I want you* and *your children.*

Travis grew serious, leaning forward, his forearms resting on his thighs. "Mei, when the time's right, we'll have that big family you've always dreamed of."

Lately, she'd compromised with herself, thinking that Isabel would be enough. But her hopes for two sons and two daughters had still wavered in the back of her mind, an abandoned mirage.

"Odd," she said, "but it seemed so natural that we would have a large family. When you're young, you don't see how much work is in store. You don't have any idea what reality is going to bring."

She went quiet, retreating into the shell that had allowed her to repress her frustration in the first place.

She'd had a lot of practice at fading into the background, withholding her true feelings because it made everything all that much easier. Although Hong Kong was cosmopolitan and operated under the influence of Western culture, she'd buried her reactions while acclimating to America, where it was nonetheless so different. She'd been educated in English as a second language, so upon coming here, her parents had enrolled her in private school, sheltering her, really, as they always had. She just hadn't realized it until she'd gone to college.

In those first years, she had been shocked by how

American kids treated authority figures, talking back, disrespecting them. So in order to fit in, she had hidden her reactions, fading into the background so as not to be singled out by anyone.

But falling in love with Travis when they were so young had encouraged her to come out in many ways.

Even so, there would always be that remaining part of her that didn't want to cause a stir—the part that had allowed her to let his savior complex get out of control.

He leaned forward, holding the sides of her legs. The contact rattled her with its intensity—raw, unrestrained passion shaking her up. She'd missed the roughness of his hands, the heat….

Mei tried to contain herself, but her voice trembled, anyway. "Sometimes I'm afraid that all we have left is this."

She gestured toward her legs, his hands.

Travis's hold on her remained strong. "There's more, Mei. A hell of a lot more."

She looked into his green-gray eyes. "It's just… When we were younger, a relationship seemed so effortless."

"Courting is the simple part, I suppose. It helped me to try and get your parents on my side, but the early days were exciting because I was learning everything about you. Your ambitions. Your culture—even though I still almost cause international incidents all the time."

He didn't have to add that it was confusing to know a lot of customs when most of the Chang relatives who lived here had adapted American attitudes and lifestyles in addition to keeping some of the old ones.

At the memories of how hard he'd always tried, wetness pricked at her eyes. But she held back. Tears were just too impossible to handle right now.

Yet at the optimism she still saw in him, she couldn't help giving in to them.

Travis reached out to wipe a tear that had fallen to her cheek. He didn't want her to be so sad. How had it gotten to the point where he did this to her?

He only wished they could rediscover what had brought them together in the first place.

But how could they avoid what was also tearing them apart?

Fire...screams...that hand reaching out...

He calmed himself, turning all of his focus to his wife.

"Do you remember," he said, "how love at first sight felt?"

Mei's smile wobbled. Their attraction had been pure. She'd never been with another man and he'd felt as if everything were so new with her, as well.

"I remember, too, just as if it was yesterday." Travis laughed at the unfettered innocence of it. "I recall the first day you reported for your college summer internship at Webb Incorporated. I was in charge of showing you around."

"The son of the boss, training to take his dad's place someday. One of the admin assistants kidded me about being careful of your reputation. A real ladies' man, she said."

"I was selective. It's just that women like a guy who hails from affluence."

"A *lot* of women."

"Then you walked into my office," he said, "so confident, vibrant and beautiful in your red business suit. You had your hair in one of those fancy buns—"

"—a chignon. I thought it looked so sophisticated—"

"—and I was floored."

Mei glanced away, cheeks pinkening. "You were horny."

"No." He gripped her legs again. "I knew you would be different from any of the others. I thought to myself, 'That's the woman I'm going to marry.' I knew right away."

He had skipped the tough parts, like how their parents weren't very supportive of their cross-cultural relationship, at first. His mom had come around, but not his dad.

Never his dad.

To him, Mei had been an employee, a girl it was okay to date but not to marry. He'd had his sights set higher in the area's social set for Travis and his two sisters.

Then there were Mei's parents. They seemed to think that their daughter was veering away from them, even though she meticulously braided the customs that made sense to her with the new ones she was discovering in her adopted country. Unfortunately, one of her inspired choices was to turn aside from the expectation that she go to work for her uncle's import company; instead, she'd ended up signing on with Webb Incorporated, after her internship had finished.

Another deviation was Travis, and even though her family and extended clan were incredibly important to her, she had followed her own heart there, too.

He leaned closer to his wife, his true love, whisper to whisper.

"You *are* the woman I'm going to spend the rest of my

life with, Mei. I knew it at twenty years old and I sure as hell know it now."

Then, unable to hold himself back any longer, he pressed his lips to hers, initiating the kiss that had been escaping them since he'd arrived.

She sucked in a breath, startled.

And when he slipped his hand to the back of her head, beneath her ponytail, he groaned.

Her hair felt sleek as it fell over his knuckles. She tasted just as intoxicating as he remembered: sweet like sugar licked off of a warm cookie.

Unable to help himself, he sipped at her, desire pushing through his veins and pulsing to his belly, his groin.

She made a tiny mewling sound, grabbing at his shirt and pulling him closer. Her urgency fogged his head, scrambling all his best intentions to take this slow.

To show her that there was more between them than the physical. That, even if he could never touch her again, he would worship her. Love her.

But hold back, he told himself. *Restrain.*

He fought hard to do so, even as his body rose in temperature and excitement. His belly churned with a mix of it, all heat and hunger.

She parted her lips, as if wanting to deepen the kiss. At first, he instinctively responded, his hand brushing down the nape of her neck—so soft—and down her shoulder, down her slender arm, then up again, to her neck, where he rubbed a thumb over her throat.

Her heartbeat pounded at him, and his breath quickened to match her rhythms.

Tied together, he thought. *Always.*

Then he thought he heard her whisper against his lips. "Travis…"

He wasn't sure if she'd really said it, because the name was lost in a blast of yearning that spiked every cell in his body.

Especially his brain.

The blast illuminated things into a freeze-frame flash: He was going too far. He would never win her over like this.

Rushing into bed after all their anguished revelations would destroy more than it would fix.

With more willpower than he'd ever imagined, he pulled back.

The physical was simple. Emotions weren't.

Surprised by this turn, he gauged Mei's reaction in the breathless aftermath.

She seemed shocked, and whether it was because of his presuming to kiss her or because of the kiss itself, he didn't know.

"It's too soon." Mei stood.

Dammit, had he blown it? Why couldn't he have waited?

"Maybe," she added, "we should get counseling before anything else. Maybe that would help most of all."

Screams…fire…

He stiffened, shutting it all out.

And, unfortunately, that included Mei.

"Why is there a need for a third party to get involved when I want to give you all the time we've been lacking together?" he asked. "Just give *me* a chance first, okay?"

Chapter Four

The next morning, Mei's eyes opened earlier than usual, but she stayed in bed, staring at the ceiling.

Trying not to remember the kiss.

But it didn't work. She kept reexperiencing the fire that exploded in her blood as Travis's lips had covered hers. The blaze of hunger consuming her as she'd responded, murmuring his name and wanting more...

Finally, she willed the sensations to stop, yet her body just wouldn't cooperate.

It throbbed, hummed, craved yet another kiss.

Travis is your husband, it insisted. *Welcome him back. Show him how much you still love him.*

Mei evened out her breathing, then slipped out of bed. Lord knew she wanted to wake up next to him, burrowing into his body, smelling his musky scent. She wanted the man she'd married, pure and simple, their promises of love still unchanged by what life had tossed their way.

But that wasn't the reality.

She got ready, got herself together. And when she pulled on a pair of jeans she hadn't worn for a few weeks, she discovered that they were pretty snug.

Going over to the mirror, she looked at her body. Looked at a tummy that wasn't quite as flat as usual.

Mei swallowed hard. What if…?

No. There was no way.

She had gone on the Pill after Isabel's birth because they'd wanted to wait for the right time to try again. Mei had even been on it the last time she and Travis had made love, before he'd left for the brush fires.

But what about this tighter clothing?

Now her dizziness and tiredness took on a whole new meaning, too. So did the fact that she hadn't gotten her period yet. But she'd thought that was because of stress.

A thought zipped through her mind. Her vanquished bronchitis and the medication she'd taken to finally wipe away the lingering symptoms.

Careless, she thought, just now remembering something vague she'd once heard about antibiotics reducing the effectiveness of the Pill….

Mind spinning, Mei traded her old jeans for a baggier pair of navy pants.

She couldn't be pregnant. Yes, she wanted more children—God, so badly—but a baby right now?

In spite of everything, a combination of excitement and anxiety crowded her while she rested a hand on her belly, and she smiled ever so slightly before allowing her hand to drop to her side.

Stress—it had to be stress, that's all. She would even buy a pregnancy test, just to put her mind at ease.

But if the results were positive, would that make her feel better or worse?

Couldn't she just concentrate on Travis, on healing their marriage, before this new curveball came their way?

As she opened her bedroom door, she told herself not to think about it. Not to hope. Not to worry.

Instead, she awakened Isabel with a big kiss, then took her daughter to the kitchen for breakfast. On the way, Mei heard Travis in the second bathroom, where he was taking a shower.

She avoided any thoughts of his body, wet and glistening under the slickness of soap and water. Then she cleaned up the remnants of Travis's rearrange-the-cupboard quest from yesterday. Sometimes he didn't finish his home projects and Mei would tie up his loose ends.

Afterward, she made oatmeal, which allowed Isabel to happily create raisin designs on the surface while Mei ate, too.

Meanwhile, she kept touching her tummy and finding herself grinning, then getting nervous....

Soon, Travis entered the dining area, his hair damp and disheveled, his face freshly shaven, his green-gray eyes shining with optimism.

Her stomach whirled.

"Morning," he said, his deep voice running over her like a caress.

As Isabel chirped a "Good morning" right back at him, Mei tried not to look at his lips.

But she did. Darn her, she couldn't help it. They'd been so warm, so welcoming last night.

She managed to pull her gaze away and collect herself. "Morning. You all rested up?"

"For what? My days of leisure?" He made his way to the kitchen, where Mei had left out a ceramic bowl for him. While he talked, he scooped oatmeal from its covered pot on the stove and washed, then sliced, an apple from the fruit basket. "Say, Izzy, how about we have a day out?"

"A day out?" Their daughter took two raisins and pretended they were her eyes, then laughed as Travis smiled at her games.

"Just you and me, kid," he continued. "We'll leave Mommy here this time so she can concentrate on working, and you can help me put together an outing for the whole family tonight."

The whole family, Mei thought, fighting the urge to touch her belly again.

Travis glanced at her, and she saw that his smile displayed that same determined promise to win her trust again.

He believed that giving his time would be the biggest sacrifice, she thought. But if the fires she saw in his eyes said anything, it was that there still wasn't a balance.

Irrational jealousy spiked her once more. His job had become a mistress of sorts. A threat.

"So you've got big plans for tonight," she said, pushing back that jealousy. *She* had Travis right now, not the darkness.

"Oh, I have big, *big* plans," he repeated, adapting a confident grin as he ate his meal at the kitchen counter.

His eyes flashed against his tanned skin, and Mei's tummy scrambled yet again. And she knew that it had nothing to do with a possible pregnancy.

He still affected her like no one else.

Spooning the last of his oatmeal into his mouth, he rinsed his bowl and utensil in the sink and put them into the dishwasher. "Just be ready by four-thirty. Dress warm. Be hungry."

Now she was intrigued. "What…?"

"I'm not telling." He came to the table and scooped Isabel into his arms while heading toward her room. Their daughter squealed and laughed, clearly blissful to have Daddy playing around like this.

"Since I've got this little monkeybug for the rest of the day," he said, "you go ahead and get your work done while we dart off to…" He paused, then addressed Isabel. "What do you think about the zoo?"

She raised her hands in the air. "I love the zoo!"

He turned to Mei. "Sound okay?"

"Sounds great."

He tossed her one last smile before disappearing into the hallway with Isabel, their laughter wrapping Mei in its echoes.

It was only when they were gone that she finally gave in to the temptation to feel the very slight curve of her belly.

This version of Travis—the one who had it in him to be so enthusiastic about being a father—was the man she thought she'd married.

But would he be here after vacation was over?

* * *

The sun balanced on the horizon, its colors softening to shades of dusk as it whisked over the picnic spread Travis had put together.

It'd been a day full of giraffe-viewing, elephant-gazing and even a little cotton-candy snacking at the zoo. A day of bonding with his daughter.

A day of realizing that he had never enjoyed much one-on-one time with Isabel like this. Sure, he'd gone out to eat dinner with her and Mei when he could, and he'd even managed to attend a few other activities with them, too, but the trips had always been shaded by a restlessness to get back to the firehouse.

In fact, he'd been so enthusiastic about making things up to Isabel that she'd fallen asleep in her car seat on the way back from the zoo. However, she'd woken when they arrived home, where he'd cooked dinner and then packed the family in the car again so they could go to the renovated drive-in park at Magnolia Point.

Back in the seventies, the Magnolia had been a thriving hot spot where cars had pulled in to see double features under a nighttime sky. However, when drive-ins had left behind their heydays, the owners had decided to construct a family-friendly destination by keeping the huge screens, replacing the dirt with no-cars-allowed grass for frolicking and picnicking, and then constructing low speaker stands to provide sound. Off to the side, they'd even put in a "sprayground" that was popular during summer days.

But right now, the September night brought a cool breeze with its sunset, and the children had turned away from the closed waterworks in favor of concentrating on the slides and the swings at the more traditional playground.

Isabel had already romped there to her satisfaction, and now she was digging into the food Travis had brought. It lifted him up to see that something like the breadcrumb-coated fried chicken, the vinegar-tinged coleslaw and the brown-sugared beans could give her just as much joy as she'd shown while eating a hot dog at the zoo.

As a probationary firefighter—or "probie"—he had shouldered the brunt of the meal-making for his shift during the last year and a half, before he'd become a regular. So he was good at it. Yet he'd rarely engaged in kitchen duty at home because Mei had always taken up the chore. She said she liked whipping up their meals, and he'd never questioned that.

But was this only one more thing he'd taken for granted—her willingness to provide for him? Shouldn't he have surprised her every once in a while with his own efforts?

Well, he was sure as hell going to do it now, and from the looks of it, she appreciated the gesture.

"So," she said after nibbling at a drumstick, "I can tell that this is all you boys do when you're not on a call—cook good meals and then eat like kings."

"Depends who pulls grub duty."

As Mei grinned, Isabel laughed.

"Grub," their daughter said. "What does that mean?"

He counted the synonyms off on his fingers. "Food. Vittles. Chow."

"Chow!" Isabel laughed again. "At school, Torrey

Morgan said she ate some of her puppy's chow. That's funny."

Mei gingerly put down her chicken and dabbed at her lips with a paper napkin. Clearly, the conversation had caused a break in appetite. She'd even gone a little pale.

He ached to smooth a finger over her cheek.

"You okay?" he asked instead.

"Sure. Fine." But her complexion contradicted that.

"Maybe," he said, flicking a finger under his daughter's chin, "we should move on and talk about more appetizing subjects. Like…"

Isabel slipped on a charming smile. "Like getting a puppy?"

First babies and now puppy dogs. Isabel obviously wanted to grow the family, but Travis wasn't sure this was a great idea at the moment—not when he and Mei were just starting to get back on track.

"You," he said to Isabel. "Last time I looked, you had a room full of puppy dogs and lions and tigers."

"Those aren't real, Daddy."

"Well, they'll have to do for now. You take good care of them, and maybe we'll work our way up to something else one day. Right, Mei?"

She was watching him closely, those shadows in her eyes.

Crap, had he run his mouth off? Maybe he shouldn't be telling Isabel that she could have pets someday without specifically discussing it with Mei first. It's just that they'd always planned to have a lively household, with children and dogs and cheer.

When had that changed?

But, God, it had. He couldn't deny it, because he had altered significantly the day his mother had died.

Isabel bounded over to hug Mei. "Oh, please, Mommy? I like doggies."

Mei blinked away the shadows and wrapped an arm around her daughter, kissing her forehead. "Honey, dogs are a big responsibility. A lot of work and care."

Her voice sounded splintered, and Travis hated that. She wasn't just talking about dogs—she was talking about *them*. Families.

"That's right, Izzy," he said. "It's not just about feeding them. You've always got to pay attention, know what they need and give it to them before they can ask."

Mei closed her eyes as she kept her face against Isabel's long, straight black hair. But their daughter didn't seem to notice her mom's anguish.

"Dogs can't ask, Daddy. They can't talk."

"But," he said, "if you watch dogs closely, you can see what they need. If you're paying attention."

His daughter seemed to take that in. Absently, she played with her mom's hair, twirling it around a tiny finger. Travis imbibed the sight, feeling a part of them, but then again, not feeling it so much at all.

Once again, he was on the outside, trying to get in....

Night was introducing a deeper darkness, so they finished off the food and packed everything away, then set up camp for the movie showing.

As Travis moved their lawn chairs into viewing position and turned on the speakers so they could hear the previews, Isabel crawled over to cuddle with her back to his chest.

Travis couldn't move for a moment; he hadn't expected his daughter to come to him.

Why? He didn't know. Any dad should've been prepared. Except for him.

For Pete's sake, when was the last time they'd even enjoyed a family outing in which Isabel had an opportunity to snuggle with him?

Just thankful for the chance, he tucked a blanket over Isabel and himself, then held his daughter, resting his cheek against her head.

Out of the corner of his eye, he saw Mei glance over, and a smile ghosted her lips before she drew her flannel blanket to cover her chest.

Their gazes connected then, and he saw a glimmer in her eyes. Tears?

Instead of saying anything, he reached over to caress her cheek. A tear fell on his finger before she raised a hand to wipe her skin.

She cleared her throat. "I guess I'm starting early for this movie."

"*Beauty and the Beast?* I just thought it might entertain Izzy."

"You know what it did to me when we saw it on one of our first dates. And don't look so innocent—we rented the video. I insisted. It was more than just a kid's movie, I said. It was a classic. It was even nominated for an Academy Award."

Her wistful smile told him that she knew tonight's film choice had been pure emotional manipulation on his part.

Okay, he wasn't ashamed to admit it. He remembered how much the story had made her laugh, made her cry.

Remembered how the experience had made him adore her only that much more.

As the movie started, he held Isabel tight, but his attention kept straying to Mei. He couldn't keep his mind off of her, especially when she didn't even make it through the film's prologue before wiping at her eyes again.

But, this time, he wondered if it was because of the tale of the unlovable beast or because she was recalling a time when they'd been able to hold hands. When they'd looked at each other openly, baring all their emotions with one glance.

Wishing he could recapture it all, Travis reached out from under his blanket and rested his hand on the back of her chair—so close, but not daring to touch her without a sign that she might welcome it.

She leaned her head back, lightly resting it against him, as if to feel that he was really there. As if to measure just how long his touch would remain.

But Travis, himself, was damned sure of the answer, even if she wasn't yet.

Much later, after Isabel was asleep in her bed, Mei and Travis walked down the hallway together, a thin chasm between them.

It was becoming a pattern, tucking in their daughter and then ending up in two different rooms. Mei wondered how long they would have to put up with the charade of him living in the same apartment while remaining separated.

Because that's what they still were—separated, no matter how many picnics they went on or how much she struggled to support her ultimatum.

Back at the drive-in, she'd come close to turning her head so her skin itself would touch his hand, but... funny. Even something so innocuous had seemed momentous, and she hadn't dared.

Then Isabel had shifted in Travis's lap, putting him in a position where he couldn't rest his hand near her anymore, and that had been that.

Now they came to the guest room first, and they paused before his doorway.

"Well," he said, his voice low and mindful of their daughter down the hall.

"Well, then." Mei smiled up at him. A smile that told him how much she appreciated his endeavors. "That was a lot of fun, so thank you."

A pause stretched between them—a blank space filled with the possibility of taking up where last night's kiss had left off.

But it was too soon. Too much.

"Good night," Mei said, stepping backward to create the relief they both needed.

"Good night, Mei."

His voice. It was so inviting, but she withstood the temptation and backed away yet another foot.

Even though frustration and disappointment seemed to flash across his gaze, he aimed one last look at her, then went into his room.

Before Mei could follow him in—her senses were screaming at her to do so—she headed for her own sanctuary.

Too soon to want more, she kept telling herself, switching on her light and shutting the door behind her.

If you let him kiss you again, you'll only be back where you started before he left.

She leaned against the door, girding herself, because if she didn't take care, she would go right back out there and forget her resolve.

Instead, she stared at her bathroom door, which stood open in a summons of a different sort. She wandered over to it, standing at the threshold and debating whether or not she should…

With a nervous burst, she went to her private drawer and opened it, digging to the back where, in all its scary glory, the kit waited.

The pregnancy test she'd purchased from the neighborhood market this afternoon.

The results could change everything.

But did she want to pressure herself into accepting him back for a reason other than the ones she already had?

Or did she yearn to know that Travis wanted to change *without* this extra incentive?

Damn her for putting them both through this, but she needed to know that he would stay the course for her and Isabel alone. She didn't know if she could take it if she suspected that they'd both forgotten the real reasons they'd drifted apart.

Shutting the cabinet door, Mei made the choice to wait.

At least, for tonight.

The terrible dream came again for Travis, just as it invaded night after night, buried in the throes of a haunted sleep.

His mom, taking a break from shopping that day, eating lunch at an indoor, third-story café with friends. Laughing, trading stories, never suspecting…

Then…fire.

The beast, seething into the room with such sudden ferocity that no one could've been prepared.

Beams falling, pinning, crushing.

A hand reaching out from the flaming debris….

Travis tried to grab that hand, but he came up short, just as he always did. Still…

One more inch, keep trying, never stop—

He woke up in a sweat, gasping, heart jackhammering through him with such force that he thought it might choke him.

A shadow by his bed, speaking urgently. "Travis? I heard you from down the hall…."

A hand on his shoulder. It was small, delicate.

Mei.

He grabbed her hand and pressed his lips to her skin, tried to calm his breathing, but adrenaline was ripping through him, sharp and cold.

"Oh, Travis." The mattress dipped as she sat on it. "The dream?"

"Yeah." The contents never changed much, so she already knew it well.

"You don't know things happened that way." Her voice was soothing, like a balm spread over a cut. "The investigation indicated that she died instantly—"

"So they say."

He tried to drive out the image of the hand, always reaching, always attempting to drag him back in its efforts to beg for help.

Mei's upturned palm tasted sweet against his mouth, and he wished that could fill him and take the place of the horror. In his peripheral vision, the shadow of her other hand wavered in the air, as if she didn't know whether to touch him or not.

But the hesitation was only momentary.

The calming weight of her fingers branded him as she smoothed back his damp hair. "It'll be okay."

He stiffened. Would it?

Would he ever stop waking up like this?

Sometimes when Travis slept away from the firehouse, he would have a toss-and-turn night. However, while on shift, he never had the nightmares—probably because he was doing something about his fears—and if the alarm sounded during slumber time, he was ready, charging to go.

She seemed to know what was going through his mind, and he felt her posture slump.

"What can I do to make it go away?" she whispered, and she wasn't just talking about right here and now.

"Just do what you're doing," he said.

She sighed, sounding as if she'd run clean out of energy.

In the quiet that followed, he could guess the rest. They both knew that his only real comfort was in fighting, in going to work and facing the nightmares that only disappeared temporarily, then came roaring back once he was out of action.

But he didn't want it to be that way anymore.

In the dark, as he held his lips against Mei's hand—trying to restrain himself as he hungered for so much more—she resumed stroking his hair.

Chapter Five

Much to Travis's surprise, he had actually gotten some sleep for the rest of the night and woken up without the demons on his back for the first time in months.

That's not to say he hadn't kicked off the blankets. But once, when he had jerked awake, he'd caught sight of Mei dozing on the bed, obviously staying near him in case of another nightmare. After that, he'd calmed down and hadn't awakened until now, when he found her gone.

Yet he hadn't minded so much, because the fact that she had stayed at all was a positive sign. Maybe that's why he was so optimistic this morning.

Travis rolled off the mattress, stretching, then going to shower. Afterward, he went to the kitchen to make breakfast, revving up the coffee machine and then scanning the contents of the refrigerator and freezer.

Not long after he'd started, a bed-headed Isabel wandered out, and the sight of her touched Travis. Their daughter was living proof of his and Mei's love, a child with his wife's dainty looks and his eyes.

"Good morning, Daddy."

He bent down to nestle Isabel into one of his arms, then stood with her, gesturing to the toaster with the other hand.

"How about some waffles?" He'd found some frozen ones and figured he would dress them up with blueberries and whipped topping.

"Can I help?"

Before he could answer, Isabel had squirmed out of his hold, wanting to be let down. He obliged her, and she headed for her bedroom, then came out with a butterfly-painted wooden step stool, which she promptly set by the kitchen counter and mounted.

How long had she been doing this? Travis didn't want to ask. He was too mortified by not knowing.

"I help Mommy all the time," Isabel said. "But I'm best at pancakes."

"You didn't want to help me yesterday?"

"No."

She did that little shrug, and Travis put a steady hand on her shoulder.

"Izzy," he said. "You know that Mommy and I love you more than anything, right?"

She nodded while trying to open the new waffle box.

Travis eased the carton away from her, hoping to get his daughter to look at him. When she did, his heart cracked.

"Your Mommy and I love each other, too," he added. "Very, very much."

She gazed at him, long and serious. Then she did the shrug again. Travis rubbed her shoulder and smiled reassuringly, even though his throat had closed around any impending words.

But Isabel took up the slack. "At school, Stacy M. doesn't have a daddy on some weekends."

"Oh, I see. Do you think I'll end up like Stacy M.'s daddy?"

She didn't say anything, and he cupped her face with his hands.

"Sweetheart," he whispered, "I don't want you to *ever* worry about that. I'm here to stay."

Her only answer was to fiercely clamp her arms around his waist, pressing her face to his stomach. He embraced her just as hard.

A few moments passed before she pulled away, smiling, going back to the waffle box while he watched, his chest aching.

He carried on with breakfast service by pouring orange juice into some plastic cups. All the same, every once in a while, he would touch Isabel's back, just to let her know he was still there.

The waffles popped out of the toaster and he placed them on plastic plates, then supervised Isabel as she put the finishing blueberry-and-topping touches on the food.

"Maybe," he said, hugging his daughter to his side as she dabbed one more mound of creamy topping on to her own waffle, "we should serve Mommy breakfast in bed. What do you think of that?"

A voice came from behind them, causing both Isabel and Travis to turn around.

"Thanks for the thought," Mei said, "but I already caught the smell of breakfast wafting in the air."

Travis's senses rushed him, all but sifting out everything but Mei, standing there in a fluffy white robe, her hair neatly fixed into a low ponytail even if her sleep-flushed face belied that she'd just gotten out of her bed.

He'd been holding his breath, and once he remembered to finally take another one, a back draft rocked Travis, a burst of fiery need so powerful that it nearly devoured him.

But how could he make *her* believe that?

From the look on Mei's face, she'd felt the same heat. He could see it in her eyes, in the way she gripped the lapels of her robe.

Or was he only projecting onto her?

While the earth was moving, the angels singing, Isabel put their breakfast on the table, then sat down and dug in, sending a grin to Travis.

He winked at her.

"Once again, you two got up earlier than usual," Mei said, going to Isabel and rubbing a finger over their daughter's cheek. "My alarm hadn't even gone off. Maybe I should get up at dawn to beat you."

"I just hear Daddy and then I get out of bed." Isabel had a spot of whipped topping near the corner of her mouth. "He was right here when I found him."

He was right here.

Travis glanced at Mei to see if she'd caught Isabel's significant comment, too. The softness in her eyes told him she had.

She lovingly wiped the food from their daughter's

face while the girl said, "I like getting up to help Daddy with breakfast."

"I like it, too," Mei said, tucking a strand of hair behind Isabel's ear before she joined Travis in the kitchen. "I can see it's becoming a nice habit for you both."

She smiled gently, reaching for the coffeepot on its burner. But for some reason, she seemed to think better of it and poured herself a glass of orange juice instead.

Riding this positive wave, Travis sauntered nearer to her. He loved how she smelled in the mornings, all sleep-warmed. Then again, he loved her scent at night, too.

Anytime.

While she took a sip from her glass, he bent toward her ear, his words tickling the stray hairs.

"What're you doing tonight, Mei?"

She finished drinking, then fixed her melting brown eyes on him. At the sight, he almost forgot himself and drew her into his arms. All he wanted to do was feel her again. Love her.

"My schedule's wide-open," she whispered.

At her low voice, he inched closer. She caught her breath.

"I want it to be just us this time," he said. "Alone."

A hint of doubt flashed over her eyes, and he realized that she might be thinking he was putting on the moves, planning a seduction to move their reunion along.

"Don't worry," he said. "I'll be a good boy."

That seemed to relax her, and she nodded, clearly ready and willing for at least that much.

"I'll call my parents so Isabel can stay with them," she said. "They were asking if they could have a sleepover this weekend, anyway."

"Then I'll take care of dinner. And don't worry about anything but getting your work done today. I'd like to spend time with Isabel before she leaves tonight."

That meant driving their daughter to and from her three-day-a-week preschool, but he also intended to take up where he'd left off with the zoo yesterday. Maybe they could go to the pizza parlor, the movies...whatever she wanted to do.

Whatever would make up for lost time.

Mei's gaze was still cautious, but he was going to put an end to that.

"Then after you get back with Isabel," she said, "I can drop her off at Mom and Dad's."

It was on the tip of his tongue to say that he could take care of that, too, but he knew how awkward it would be to see Mr. and Mrs. Chang without Mei there. Normally, their meetings were semiawkward at best. Plus, he assumed Mei had been making more excuses to them about his longer-than-usual absence, and that wouldn't go over well.

He would see them another time, after both he *and* Mei felt more comfortable with their own situation.

"Sounds like a plan." Then he lowered his voice, the tone in itself a promise. "Tonight, then?"

And from the way her hand trembled as she raised her juice glass to her lips, he knew that she'd recognized that promise, too.

After dropping his daughter off at her preschool—where the aides welcomed him with beaming smiles and the kids looked at him with awe while Isabel bragged about her "firedad"—Travis fully intended to go to the hardware store so he could buy supplies for those shelves he'd always meant to build in the family room. Afterward, he would fetch Isabel and they would have their fun before he stopped by the market, then took her home.

But it didn't quite happen like that.

Somehow, he found himself slowing down as he passed his firehouse, which was on the way to the hardware store.

And, somehow, he found himself pulling into the parking lot and cutting the engine.

His regular crew was on right now, so...hell, why not? He had a few minutes. He would pop his head in and stay only long enough to say hi, then scram.

That's all he would do.

Yet as he climbed out of his pickup, he knew better. After he'd left Isabel at school, the atmosphere in the cab had been silent, and his nightmare had crawled back to him, leaping on him and injecting him with a shot of nerves.

But being here, in front of the two-story brick structure that felt like another home, his heartbeat was already soothed, his mind calm.

And when he strolled up to the open door of the apparatus floor and saw a couple of his comrades inspecting the equipment on the engine, Travis slipped back into the skin of the man in utter control—the fighter who didn't have nightmares.

"Well, look at this," said a beefy man with a handlebar mustache as he backed away from the rig. Andy McCorkle, the engineer on shift. "You couldn't stand to be away from all the abuse, could ya?"

Another firefighter waved Andy off. Jed King was a

young, wiry fellow with spiked blond hair and the strength of a bull. He'd been the one to recently put Travis up at his place before Travis had approached Mei again.

"Knock it off, McCorkle. Trav doesn't take probie crap anymore." Jed laughed while wiping his hands on a rag before he stuffed it into his dark pants. "Not when we've got new ones to harass."

In the background, a redheaded rookie nicknamed "Opie" was performing a hazing ritual Travis had been made all too familiar with when he'd come to Station Four: scrubbing the apparatus floor. It would get dirty again within seconds, but it was part of a probie's bottom-of-the-totem-pole welcome to this particular firehouse.

"Aren't you glad you're not one of them no more?" Andy asked.

"Ecstatic." Travis could do without the daily drills, the constant evaluations and the basic guff he'd been put through as a new fighter. "Then again, I kind of miss all the tender love and care you old-timers lavished on me."

Andy made a grunty disgusted sound and waved Travis off as he left to resume checking the axes, the Halligan bars, the pike poles. Jed made cooing noises just to get the veteran's goat, too.

Travis laughed, so at ease that he actually felt guilty. He wished laughter came this easily with Mei nowadays.

So what was he doing here when he should be making that happen?

Jed elbowed him. "Some vacation you must be having. Bored already?"

"Not by a long shot." Travis shrugged, stepping onto the floor, looking around at the engine, then the pole right near it. Hell, he loved that pole—loved whisking down it so he could climb into his gear and get into the jump seat of the rig on the way to a call. Station Two, where he had decided to transfer, was so small—only one story high—it didn't require a pole.

Unsettled at the notion of having to give even something that insignificant—yet so important to his psyche—up, Travis tried to ban it from his mind.

Still, it lingered.

"So what're you doing hanging around this dump?" Jed asked.

Travis didn't have a good explanation, and his friend nodded.

"Addict," Jed said.

Travis backed up a step, as if kicked with the truth.

But…damn. Maybe he wasn't so much addicted to adrenaline as he was to fixing something that couldn't be repaired.

He crossed his arms over his chest, thinking about Mei's ultimatum, thinking about what it might be like not to have this job. He'd be numb.

Frozen if he couldn't fight back.

His gut flip-flopped as realization upon realization attacked.

After his mom's death…he'd distanced himself from everyone who mattered.

Even Mei.

By removing himself—emotionally and otherwise—he'd effectively made sure he wouldn't lose another person he loved, even while he thought he was trying to save everybody….

Sweat started to mist his skin.

He wouldn't mention any of this to Jed. In fact, he'd never told any of the men about his motivations for being here. He'd even avoided talking about this pain that never seemed to abate as much as he could during the interviewing process.

He could fix himself all on his own.

Tightly laughing off Jed's comment, Travis said, "Addict, my ass."

"Aw." His friend cocked a brow. "Come on, Trav. Tell me your feelings. Let it all go, just like they keep asking us to do around here."

He merely brushed Jed off, never showing how close to the bone the other man was sawing. In the aftermath of 9/11, head doctors had become a fixture, readily available to the county's emergency workers. But therapy was a sign of weakness around the firehouse, with all its machismo.

Was that why he'd displayed such a knee-jerk reaction to Mei's suggestion that *they* seek help?

By this time, Opie had wandered over, scrub brush in hand. "Hey, there, Webb. What're you doing around this—"

Before he had to answer the question a second time, Travis jerked his chin back to where his pickup was parked. "Just on my way to the hardware store when I decided to drop by to see you public servants sweating it out."

Jed started backing onto the apparatus floor. "Sure. You only missed your sweethearts, that's all."

Travis stuck his hand in the air as a succinct farewell and walked back to his truck.

Because when all was said and done, his sweethearts were at home, and they were the ones he needed to get back to.

Later, after Mei had taken Isabel to her folks' house, she walked back into the apartment to find the place transformed.

At least, she hadn't seen it this way in years.

As she wandered inside, a glow of soft light greeted her—candles contained in small lanterns she'd once bought on a whim. They were placed around the dining area, around the table set with their best Delft china and a centerpiece bowl filled with water and rose petals.

Mei dropped her purse near the kitchen counter, her heart going to her throat.

This was evidence of Travis's all-too-persuasive romantic streak: the way he used to surprise her just after they got married with wine and cheese on a bench by the bay. The way he used to sweep her off at the end of a workweek when they were both at Webb Incorporated, to a B and B in the mountains or a weekend trip to a fancy hotel.

He stepped out from behind the long pantry cupboard, dressed casually in jeans and a white T-shirt that was minus any of his usual mischievous slogans.

So handsome with his ocean-tinted eyes clear against sun-burnished skin. So tall and rugged and strong....

"I finished lighting all these things just minutes ago," he said. "My timing is *on*."

He seemed to want to inject some lightness into the evening, but she could tell there was something behind that gorgeous gaze. A heaviness.

"Dinner smells wonderful." She smoothed down the airy long-sleeved yellow dress she'd donned earlier. She wanted to look nice tonight, wanted things to go well, even if a true reunion couldn't happen yet.

Not until she was more secure in his promises—and until she could ascertain how the future might affect the child who might be growing within her.

"So," he said, "how are your mom and pop?"

"Over the moon to see Isabel, of course."

Travis nodded, busying himself by readying a bottle of wine.

Mei held up a hand. "None for me, thanks. I don't have a yen for it tonight."

"Then," he said with a smile, clearly not suspecting her real reason for avoiding alcohol, "I hope you don't mind if I grab a beer."

"Have at it."

As he opened the fridge and traded the wine for his preferred beverage, he said, "I imagine you told your parents I'm back."

Great—this was not how she'd wanted their night to start out, but she would be honest.

"I'd already mentioned it, so it wasn't a surprise."

"And they proceeded to remind you about what a mistake you made by marrying me, the boy from a snobby family. The guy who'd never come to any good."

Mei walked over to the kitchen counter and leaned on it. "Okay, their tune hasn't changed—it's just gained a new chorus."

He fished in the utensil drawer for a bottle opener, popped open his beer and saluted her. "You said that with a real impressive flourish, Mei. Now, that's how to put a spin on something."

"I wasn't in marketing for nothing." She traced the edges of the white counter tiles. "You know my parents are always going to be a challenge. They had their eye on a perfect son-in-law once we came to America, and I disappointed them by going against their plans. You started out with a disadvantage, Travis, and…"

She trailed off.

But he picked right back up where she'd ended. "And I didn't do much to prove you'd made the right choice in a devoted husband."

"That was then, and this is now," she said hopefully.

He looked at her still-bare ring finger, and that said it all.

She lowered her hand from the counter, picturing her wedding band waiting in the vanity drawer in the bedroom, where it seemed lonely in its velvet-box vigil.

Taking a deep breath, she gestured toward the stove, where covered pots and pans gleamed in the dimness. "What's cooking?"

He seemed dissatisfied at the reprieve. "Garlic mashed potatoes and leeks to go with some sautéed scallops. Your favorite meal, followed by some chocolate mousse."

Scallops. She did love them, but not if she were pregnant. She didn't want to take any chances with seafood.

He went over to the table and pulled out her chair. She took it, grinning at him. In spite of everything, Travis would never stop being a gentleman.

As she adjusted her skirt, she felt him standing over her. Felt the heat of his skin, the overwhelming awareness of just being near him. And then…something more.

His hand on her hair.

One stroke.

One tentative step toward a more intimate reconciliation.

Her core went hot, desire melting down until it stirred low and tingling.

Travis knew just how to touch her.

Glancing up at him, she wanted to make it clear that tonight was just about talk, and talk only, but she couldn't speak.

His eyes were a murky green, clouded with darkness, and a quiver of fear jumbled her already muddled senses.

"I went to the firehouse today," he said softly.

A leaden weight settled on her. "Why?"

"I…" He shook his head. "The nightmare dogged me when I had time to think about it, and I just found myself there while I was running errands."

She wouldn't cry. Wouldn't do it now, even if she couldn't seem to help it anymore.

"And here I thought we were getting somewhere," she said, the words catching on their way out.

"We are." He kept his hand near her hair, as if he wanted to stroke it again but didn't know if he should. "I told you because I had to be honest. But I left quickly, right after I realized it's not where I wanted to be."

Should she believe him?

"It's as if you can't help yourself." She looked down at the table. "It's as if you need more than just…me."

As the question hovered, she tried to chase away the looks on her parents' faces earlier. Among other questions, she knew they'd probably already asked themselves the exact same thing: why wasn't Mei able to keep her husband home?

Worst of all, she knew they thought that a mate they approved of would've appreciated their daughter more if she had only followed their advice.

"Oh, hey, now," Travis said, sounding upset, too. "Mei, you know you're the best wife a man could ever ask for."

She didn't want to meet his eyes, because if she did, she would lose it. The last thing they needed was tears, because their situation required logic at this point. Emotion would get them into deeper trouble.

Yet it didn't require more than a tender touch, his fingers underneath her chin, to guide her gaze back to him.

"Mei," he said again, but this time it was just a whisper.

Soft, low, tempting.

A laden beat passed, filled with such repressed longing that her heart began, pounding, pounding. Demanding.

Before she knew it, they were inches apart. Heartbeats.

A breath.

Yes, she thought. *Yes*.

And then their lips met, just as she'd been craving all along.

Chapter Six

As Travis kissed his wife, he groaned, reveling in how Mei tasted.

In having her become a part of him once again.

Her lips were a touch salty, as if the unshed tears gleaming in her eyes had already fallen and coated her mouth with moist sorrow. Moved by that, he kept drinking her in, slowly running his thumb down her cheekbone, reacquainting himself with the woman he never should've left.

When she made a small sound of need, he slid a hand to the small of her back, then the other one to the back of her head, where he buried his fingers in her sleek hair.

She didn't resist, as he had feared she might. In fact, she grabbed on to his shirt, holding on for dear life while she parted her lips underneath his, welcoming him further.

But he didn't press on. No, he merely deepened the soft, sweet rhythm of his mouth on hers. He stroked her jawline, her throat, feeling the warm skin that he had only been able to touch in his fantasies lately.

While he'd been away, cutting fire lines, every restful moment had been filled with thoughts of Mei: how her shiny hair felt when it slid through his fingers, how her petite figure fit so right against his bigger body. It was as if she'd been the sustenance he'd needed to keep fighting—water quenching an unending thirst.

Now he luxuriated in the reality of actually holding her, feeling her, having her.

Short of breath, he rested his mouth against her neck, absorbing the bang of her pulse. He kissed her there, his own blood pumping through him and driving him to go on.

But during the searing pause, Mei sucked in her own breath—a big, abrupt one—and loosened her fevered hold on his shirt.

She was regaining her equilibrium.

Dammit, he would only go further if she wanted it, heart *and* head. Getting physical—no matter how much he was aching to—would only complicate things.

Gathering himself, he pulled back, cupping her face in his hands, unwilling to fully let go. She was so beautiful it hurt.

"Any man would die to have you as his wife," he said, adding one last reassurance to her comment about her not being enough to sustain him.

"I'm still afraid because…" Closing her eyes, she leaned into one of the hands he held against her face. "Do you remember when we made promises to each other the first time?"

"When we fell in love and I told you we'd be happy forever?"

"Yes. And then during the tea ceremony."

How could he forget? Mei had really wanted to work elements of the Chinese tradition into their nuptials. So he'd easily agreed, knowing how much it meant to her. Besides, he'd especially liked the part about bargaining for his bride. The door game, harkening back to ancient times, was based on the premise that the bride's family and friends didn't want to see her married off. Being stopped at the door by Mei's friends and good-naturedly ribbed about what he would give for her had been romantic and fun, and it had given him a chance to show Mei just how valuable she was to him.

So why had he ever stopped?

Smoke seemed to filter into his head, ironically illuminating the answer rather than obscuring it.

Travis's hands fell away from her face, down to her shoulders, which seemed far too fragile to be holding all the troubles he'd put there.

"Mei, I'm sorry for breaking those vows. I never meant to."

"I know, but that saddens me just as much. I should've been more vocal about it sooner."

Without thinking, he tightened his grip on her shoulders, then released his hold altogether. "None of this lies on you. Do you understand that? It's all on me. Every single bit of it."

Mei's eyes took on a fire of their own, and she leaned toward him.

"No, Travis. We're in this together. You, me, Isabel…" She faltered, but then gripped his hands and held them in front of her in a position that almost reminded him of a communal prayer. "All of us."

For the first time in years, something seemed to give, just like a door bursting open after he'd been kicking at it in vain.

Unable to speak, he leaned his forehead against their clasped hands. Mei joined him, and they stayed like that.

Finally on their way to a new beginning.

During dinner, Mei felt as if she were still vibrating, her lips—her entire body—trembling from that kiss.

Several times she even touched her mouth, as if to keep the sensation fresh and alive, but her head was doing a good job of that on its own. It kept replaying the joy of being with him: the scratch-burn of his face on her skin, the slight hint of beer as he had brushed his lips over hers.

She had been repressing the ache for him for so long that the actual moment of contact had almost been too much for her to handle. But they needed to rebuild what had been worn down from a neglect that had crept up slowly yet definitely.

Now, after he'd cleared away the salad plates, sautéed the scallops and then brought the main course to the table, Mei could see the first rays of success lighting over them, just as bright as the candle flames wavering against the white walls.

Even so, past experience still cast a few shadows.

Mei took a sip of water. She wouldn't be negative, especially if that pregnancy test in her drawer ended up reading positive.

Travis had plated her food and set it in front of her. "You sure about the scallops? How about I cook up something else for you?"

"That's okay. I think I'm not in the mood for meat tonight, either." Just like she hadn't been up for the wine. "Those side dishes look great, though."

She would sneak some protein later, because putting him through more work didn't seem right.

Sitting down, he seemed concerned. "Are you sure you're not getting sick again? I know you were well on your way to getting over that bronchitis when I left, but that wouldn't affect your appetite."

"No, really, I'm fine. Maybe it's my palate or whatever. It could be changing. Doesn't that happen as you get older?"

She had no idea what she was saying in this scramble to avoid telling him about her baby suspicions. Let them work on the basics first. Let them see if there was a chance for them to reunite because they loved each other, not because they felt compelled to be together out of heightened duty.

He'd shrugged at her question. Who knew about palates?

But to make up for not eating the scallops he'd so thoughtfully cooked for her, she had her fill of the mashed potatoes and leeks. And she would sure partake of the chocolate mousse. No problems there.

"This is fantastic, Travis," she said, her mouth singing with the perfectly seasoned vegetables. "Who knew you would turn into such a great cook?"

"It wasn't really a choice." He heartily washed some of

the food down with beer. "Firehouse life kind of gives you a crash course in grocery shopping and grub wrangling. And with the cutback in volunteer hours, I'll be making good use of our kitchen. I'll cook on my days off, and Isabel can help if she wants to. I'd really like it if she did."

Mei's skin flushed as she thought of the future. Would there be another child—or more—running around while Isabel was cooking up a storm?

Boys?

Girls?

Soreness surrounded her heart, and she stirred the potatoes on her plate in an attempt to combat the effect.

He clearly read her anxiety, yet he couldn't have known the real reason for it. "Enough of the firehouse talk."

"No, Travis. I *like* to hear about the practical jokes and what you do during your downtime around the station." She left out the fact that they both knew he didn't talk about the gritty details of the job itself. Not hearing about what he faced out there was an unspoken agreement that many of the other wives subscribed to, as well. It kept them all sane.

"Nah." He grinned and took another stab at his meal. "There's a lot more we can talk about. Like…well, years ago, what did you imagine for us at this point in our marriage?"

Bliss, she thought. A full life with the man she loved.

"I imagined you running Webb Incorporated, hand in hand with your dad by now," she said, watching him closely. "I pictured me quitting the marketing game to be a stay-at-home mom, devoting myself to the kids. After I met you, I realized the most important job was raising our family. Nine-to-five turned out not to be my thing, anyway. Not when I realized early on that I'd gain more fulfillment at home than at an office."

Travis set down his fork, then stared into one of the candle lanterns he'd placed on the table, but as far as he knew, she'd been talking about Isabel, not necessarily the child they might be having.

She bit her lip, stopping herself from telling him, even if her heart was insisting on it.

"If someone would've predicted that my dad and I would hardly be talking after Mom passed on," he said, "I would've said they were nuts."

"Things change." Mei played with a leek on her plate. "We adjust. Ideals get bent and we follow their new directions."

"Just like we had to."

"Right," she said. "There always comes a point when young love has to mature."

He'd stopped eating by now, pushing his plate away so he could lean his elbows on the table. His attention was all hers.

She soldiered on. "Life throws things our way. Tough things. And there's no shame in not being able to handle them on our own."

"Are we talking about therapy again?"

"Why not?"

She reached out her hand to take his, but he fisted his own, resisting.

He'd shut her out of whatever was going on inside of him, and she didn't know what to do.

How could she whenever he became a man she didn't recognize anymore?

He seemed to realize what he'd done, and he smiled at her, putting his hand over hers, and for a moment, she told herself everything *would* work out.

But even as she turned her hand over to clasp his fingers, the shadows danced on the walls, refusing to leave.

The next morning Mei went to the Laundromat, even though it was a Saturday and her soap opera wasn't airing. Yet she'd called Jenny, who lived nearby, too, in the hopes her friend would be available for a chat.

Much to Mei's relief, the other woman said yes. Actually, the businesswoman had to make an account-maintenance trip and she'd planned to get some last-minute laundry done before her plane left tonight, anyway.

When Mei walked into the Suds Club, a basket of darks in her arms—might as well get a load done while she was here—she found Jenny in a most unsurprising place: across from Liam McCree, who was planted in his usual corner with his computer on his lap.

Jenny was shaking her head while McCree grinned; he was obviously enjoying baiting her with one feisty subject or another.

They both spotted Mei coming through the door, and just like a kid who'd been caught with her hand in the cookie jar, Jenny strolled away from him and toward a table where her dried delicate wash load was piled.

Jenny didn't ever like to admit she talked with McCree, even if she did it all the time.

"Morning, sunshine," she said to Mei.

She looked spiffy, dressed in red pants that hugged her curves and an elbow-length pink sweater that made her fifties-starlet hair seem all the softer and more stylish. Mei could've felt inferior in her own stay-at-home-mom sweats—neat but hardly for the catwalk—but she didn't. Not when she liked being that mom so much.

"What cruel force of nature has put you two in the same empty room together?" Mei asked.

"A bad roll of the dice," Jenny answered.

McCree chuckled, running a hand over his devilish goatee. "I was just making Ms. Hunter here an offer she shouldn't refuse."

"But I did, anyway," Jenny said.

Mei welcomed this distraction; every Wednesday, when Jenny had her work-from-home-day lunch hour, she spent it at the club. That meant there were plenty of fireworks between these two on display. Lord help them if they ever realized they adored each other.

"And what was this offer, McCree?" Mei asked as she prepped a washing machine for her load.

Jenny jumped in, discreetly turning her back on the man as she folded a hot little mint-colored slip. "Once again, he's only teasing me about working for that emerging Internet solutions company of his."

"She *would* work well under me," he said.

Shooting him an annoyed glance, Jenny parried. "Even if a company existed, I'd turn him down. Can you imagine a boss like that?"

"*If* the company existed?" McCree said, utterly ignoring the barb Jenny had inserted at the end. He motioned around the Laundromat. "Hey, do you not see my office? Six days a week, right here."

He paused, then added, "And I'd be a great boss."

"You're too shiftless to rent out a real space, McCree. That does not impress."

"Darlin', I'm just not comfortable in a contained space. I need a little noise and activity to keep the juices flowing."

Denying him further engagement, Jenny completed her folding and came over to Mei, who had just finished loading her darks. "Want some drinks to go with our conversation?"

As if realizing they might need some privacy, McCree put in some earbuds connected to his iPod. Not that Mei talked to him all that much, but once he'd told her that he often listened to financial podcasts.

Assured of some privacy now, Mei started toward the beverage machine. The two women had to pass McCree to get to it, so they didn't start talking until they had their drinks and were on the other side of the room, where it would be harder for him to hear.

They sat in the chairs in front of the TV, which was on very low volume while a CNN newscaster mouthed his lines.

"So how goes life?" Jenny said, starting off casually.

Mei sent her friend an appreciative grin. "It's…better with Travis lately."

Jenny was giving her a doubtful look. "That's not convincing."

"Things *have* improved. It's just that… I mean…" Mei sighed. "We're not exactly on the regular path yet. But he's working his butt off to get there."

A raised eyebrow. "Girl, you and Travis aren't getting any sexy time, are you?"

"Shh," Mei said, glancing at McCree in his corner.

But he was tapping away at his computer, his forehead furrowed as if in deep concentration.

She turned back to Jenny. "Sex is out of the question until we have everything straightened out."

"I have to agree. Sex changes everything. That's why I'm selective."

True. Although Jenny was a serial dater, she didn't sleep around.

"But," Mei said, "that doesn't mean I don't fantasize about it hourly. It's hard, Jen."

"I can imagine."

"I want to give him another chance, but…"

"You're afraid." When Jenny said it, it sounded so reasonable.

"And there's my family, too," Mei said. "Deep down, I want to show them that I made the right choice with Travis, and I think this is my opportunity to wipe the slate clean and present them with my new, improved husband." She toyed with the lid of her bottle. "I've got to get over this need for their approval."

"I understand," Jenny said, her blue eyes sympathetic. "I wouldn't want to disappoint my parents, either. And I can see why you're afraid your marriage is going to go back the way it was if you give in to your hormones this early. By rewarding him with sex, you're saying things are fine and dandy."

"You understand, then."

Phew. Now, if she could only convince her libido of the same thing.

"Sure I do," Jenny added. "I saw how his absences

affected you, and from what I can tell, it seems as if your ultimatum has shaken some sense into him."

"You truly think he's changed?"

Jenny hesitated. "I guess you'll find that out soon enough. But you're doing everything I'd do, Mei."

"Would you…" Mei's voice fell to a whisper. "Would you tell him if you thought you were pregnant?"

"Whoa." Jenny sat back in her chair. "You don't know for sure yet?"

"I've got a test waiting at home for me."

"Then take it. How can you stand not knowing?"

"Easy." Mei pushed a lost strand of hair from her ponytail away from her face. "Not knowing allows me to put off a decision. If it's true, I don't want to tell him yet."

"Because you want him to win *you* over. You don't want there to be another reason."

Thank God for Jenny. Could she have a better friend?

They kept talking for about a half hour longer, so involved that when Mei next glanced at McCree, his iPod was gone. But Mei didn't really process that; she didn't even come to any more conclusions. Jenny was a sounding board, not an expert, yet she definitely helped.

Helped a lot.

Eventually, though, her friend had to leave. "Time to pack up, since my plane won't wait for me."

"Listen, I really appreciate this." Mei stood at the same time Jenny did and hugged her. "Travel safe, okay?"

"Who me?" The other woman pulled back and beamed at Mei. "I live under a lucky star."

After Jenny left, Mei realized she hadn't been paying any attention to her laundry, so she switched her wash to a dryer. All the while, her back was to McCree, who still lingered in his corner.

Yet while she wasn't minding him, she overheard him pack up and start heading for the door.

At the sound of footfalls, she became aware of his exit, then turned to say goodbye. However, when she faced him, he stopped in his tracks, his skin going ruddy as he carried his computer in its case.

He was limping.

Awkwardly, Mei glanced away, so as not to stare. She had forgotten because, most days, he was in that chair when the club came in and still there when they left. And if he ever did walk in front of them, it was on good days, when whatever injury he had wasn't obvious.

He never talked about it, always took pains to hide it, so Mei did him the favor of acting as if she hadn't noticed.

"See you Monday?" she asked.

McCree—no longer so carefree or teasing—only nodded and headed out the door, looking chagrined to have been caught when all he'd been trying to do was sneak out.

As Mei continued folding, she realized that maybe she wasn't so different from McCree. After all, hadn't *she* been hiding all her own problems in a silent corner, too?

She touched her belly, thinking of the pregnancy test waiting for her back home.

Chapter Seven

After last night's dinner with Mei, Travis was more determined than ever to keep making progress.

He was even certain they wouldn't need anything like therapy, which was akin to admitting they had given up on trying to work things out themselves.

Self-reliance—it was what his parents had always preached. Carrie, his older sister, had caught her husband cheating but had whipped him right back into shape on her own. And his younger sibling, Julia, had found herself single and pregnant, but she had managed to persuade her ex-boyfriend to tie the knot all by herself. Even his mom and dad had once refused to ask help from anyone beyond family when their business had hit some bumps; instead of borrowing money from an astute associate who had guessed the status of Webb Incorporated, and offered to help, they had instead labored extra hours, working their fingers to the bone, until they'd crept back into the red again.

Yes, it had *all* stayed in the family, mostly because his mother had been big on discretion.

Hence, Travis now forged on with his own plans, driving steadily toward success.

And, maybe, in the back of his mind, he believed that he might do the Webbs proud this way. Maybe his dad would even appreciate Travis' solidness....

So thinking, he'd made arrangements for the family to go to the Placid Valley Children's Theater tonight. There, a midafternoon showing of *Peter Pan* kept Isabel enthralled, and Travis had been surprised at just how much he enjoyed the glow on his daughter's face during the performance.

Something had niggled at him afterward, though, and he couldn't put his finger on it.

Yet once they went to dinner, he began to understand.

After entering Isabel's favorite restaurant, Chang's Palace—owned by a member of Mei's extended family— the little girl darted over to the mahogany hostess stand, where two women were going over the reservation book.

Mei's first cousin, Li, looked up, then spread out her arms in an enthusiastic welcome. She was American-born and very much a "modern Western woman," as she liked to say.

As she hugged Isabel, her bobbed black hair shifted forward. Strands of silver loaned the woman a mature elegance, as did the classy gold dragon-and-phoenix-patterned dress she wore.

"My best customer!" Li said, hugging Isabel even tighter.

With boundless excitement, the four-year-old pulled away and then pointed at a doll in a glass case that was kept just above the computer register. The figure was wearing layers of long silks in rainbow hues, sporting flowers in her upswept hair and holding what looked to be a colorful piece of paper.

"A new doll?" Isabel asked the older woman.

"Yes." Li rose as she winked at Mei and Travis. "Her name is Jia Xichun, and she's a figure from Chinese literature. As you can see, she's holding a picture. She enjoyed painting and was very good at it."

"She's beau-ti-ful," Isabel carefully enunciated.

A party of four came through the double doors and the other hostess led them to their table. Meanwhile, Isabel wandered closer to Jia Xichun's case, staring reverently up at it.

The encased dolls that were spread throughout the entire restaurant served as a fascinating draw for her. Before Travis had left, Isabel had started asking time and again for her own, but Mei had so far only bought their daughter dolls that were age-appropriate and not meant for serious collecting.

As Isabel heaved out a dramatic sigh clearly designed to show them how much she wanted such an exquisite gift, Travis and Mei exchanged grins.

And he wouldn't have traded that moment—the unspoken words between him and his wife, the adoration of his daughter—for anything.

That's when the niggling in the back of his mind returned.

You've been investing time in them, it said, *but it's not about the hours you put in, it has to be more. Don't you feel it?*

A truth shook him: being with his family was about *relating* to Isabel and Mei more.

But had he ever truly done that?

Travis's grin dissipated, his gaze intensifying until Mei's expression changed, too. Connected, as if a wire were still holding them together, even after all the damage.

He could do it. Would do it.

Her lips parted, and he fought to keep his distance here, in front of everyone.

Dammit, he wanted to be inside her, mentally... physically.

The inner voice returned. *And when are* you *going to let* her *in?*

Li's voice interrupted. "So nice to see you all here."

Both Travis and Mei came out of it at the same time, then turned toward Mei's cousin. Travis's pulse buzzed, and he wished he could go back to burying himself in that bonded glance that had eluded them for so long.

"Yes," Mei said to Li. "I haven't seen you in...what? A week?"

The extended Chang family made it a point to get together about two to three times a month—at Golden Gate Park, at different homes, at Placid Valley's gazebo-dotted park... The venues varied, but the expectation to attend never did.

Mei accepted Li's hug, yet Travis stood back. He himself hadn't been to this restaurant for a couple of months, and he wasn't sure how to act with Li right now. Like the rest of the family, she had always been kind, but he wondered if Mei ever elaborated to them in private about how troubled her marriage had been.

Still, he knew most of her relatives would never be rude to him, even if they agreed with Mei's parents about her marrying Travis in the first place.

After Li was done hugging Mei, he waited for a sign that she was coming to hug him, then he gathered the older woman in his arms when she did.

"Good to see you, Li," he said.

She patted him on the back, then retreated enough to inspect him while still holding on to his arms.

"I guess you've been busy for a while," she said. "I tell you, this summer has been a bad one. Not much rain. Altogether too dry."

"He came back as soon as he was able," Mei said.

He felt himself flush at her quickness in making an excuse. Was she only saving face?

Thank God Isabel chimed in.

"I'm soooo hungry," she said, charging past a lacquered mahogany-and-elm wood room divider that depicted several ladies wandering in a forest.

Li grabbed a few menus, sent Travis and Mei a well-look-at-Little-Miss-in-Charge glance and led them into the seating area, too.

In the Saturday-dinner-crowded room where bamboo-pipe music played over the sound system, they sat in a rounded booth, underneath a scarlet-cloth lantern that boasted fringes and bucolic scenes. Around them, more Chinese dolls posed in their glass cases.

"Would you like menus tonight?" Li asked, brandishing them. "Or will it be the usual for all of you? Travis, even though you haven't been here in a while, I haven't forgotten what you normally order."

He grinned, trying to ignore the slight dig about his poor attendance. "I've always got a hankering for those boneless spareribs of yours."

He didn't add that Mei's home-cooked version was his favorite, though.

"And rollies?" Isabel asked, meaning the vegetable spring rolls she loved as she clapped her hands and sat on her knees. "And dumplins and chow mein?"

He was of the mind to give his daughter whatever she wanted, of course, but before he could acquiesce, Mei asked Isabel to sit like a lady would. Then she took a little coloring book and crayons out of her purse, much to Isabel's delight.

Their daughter got to work, sticking the tip of her tongue out of her mouth, inspiring Mei to run a finger over Isabel's cheek. Then she ordered from the list the little girl had recited. Since dishes were served family-style, they would share.

A waitress came by and Li rattled off the order in their Cantonese dialect. When the young woman was gone, promising to be right back with tea, Li stayed; as an owner, she had the luxury of talking with the customers and working the floor.

"Travis," she said, "when you called to tell us you were coming in tonight, Tommy and James wanted to be here, too." Tommy was her nineteen-year-old son, and James, her husband. "They went to a father-son awards dinner for James's Kiwanis Club."

During any family gatherings Travis could attend, Tommy gravitated toward him. The teen loved to ask questions about the job, and Travis found the young man to be a saving grace during what was otherwise a taut social experience.

"Sorry we missed them," Travis said. "How're they doing?"

"Same." Li nodded toward Mei. "James still wishes Tommy would be like this one. You know, focused on college and then maybe even a graduate degree. But he talks about firefighting, just like you."

Mei smiled, but Travis could see there was a line of tension holding her mouth in position. "I never did get any graduate degrees, Li."

"You intended to when you were Tommy's age. And your father? Why, he expected it—not that what you've accomplished is in any way shameful, Mei. You're a successful mother *and* you're bringing up your own business, as well. But to James and your dad, those diplomas and certificates mean the world."

While Li continued talking about Tommy, Travis could see how his wife's shoulders drooped ever so slightly.

Chest folding into itself, he instinctively reached under the table and threaded his fingers through hers. She squeezed his hand, then ran a thumb over his.

Travis shivered, his arm so close to hers that the hairs riding his skin stood on end.

Damn…One month of not being with her.

One everlasting month.

As a large party made its way to the rear room, Li excused herself, saying she would see them at the next gathering—a surprise birthday party for one of Mei's nieces that would take place tomorrow night.

In the meantime, Isabel kept coloring away, in her own little bird-and-flower world, so Travis leaned over to Mei. At the same time, he kept hold of her hand.

"Cousin Li can be direct, can't she?" he said, going for some relief to take the remaining edge off.

She seemed to appreciate that and leaned over, nestling her forehead against his shoulder. His heart seemed to jump.

"I suppose I should be used to it," she said. "There's no shortage of opinions in my family."

Travis rested a hand on top of her head, loving the feel of her hair against his palm. Silky. "You know that holds true for mine, too."

Isabel busted in. "Does Grandpa Webb have 'pinions, too?"

So she *had* been listening to their chatter about Li. And even though he doubted Isabel knew exactly what "'pinions" were, she was still a rascal.

Travis answered. "He's the emperor of opinions."

"Does he talk lots?" Isabel continued.

He wondered just how much his daughter even recalled about the grandpa she only saw about once a year. "You tell me, Izzy. Do you remember visiting him last Christmas?"

Their daughter nodded. "He gave me lots of puzzles."

Travis was surprised she had *that* much of a memory for his dad at all, seeing as they merely dropped by for the holidays more out of guilt-ridden duty than anything.

It's just that a single afternoon seemed to be the longest Charles Webb could tolerate seeing Travis and Mei together, even though he did treat Isabel with a polite, curious affection when she was around.

Travis had never analyzed it—hadn't cared to, really. But was his dad's quiet kindness to Isabel his way of offering an olive branch of sorts? Was he just too proud to take a bigger step and ask his only son to visit more often?

Worst of all, had Travis been neglecting *that* side of his life, as well?

Once again, the thought of his mother slammed him. He hadn't wanted to lose anyone else he was close to. Couldn't bear it, so he'd created distance....

Shaken, he slipped an arm around Mei.

Isabel went back to coloring, and Travis glanced down at his wife. He caught her watching him with a tender, speculative glint in her eyes, but he could tell she was still stricken by what Li had so casually mentioned about her father's disappointment.

"No matter what anyone else says," he whispered over the mumbling dining talk around them, "*I'm* damned proud of you."

Judging by the way she smiled softly at his sincere comment, pumping his veins with such affection he wasn't sure he could contain it, he guessed that she knew he meant it with all of his heart.

After arriving home, they tucked Isabel in bed among all her stuffed animals.

She wanted to hear a story about Peter Pan, so Mei and Travis put on a little show, with her using a nearby Piglet as a substitute for Tinker Bell, and him grabbing Kermit the Frog so he could engage in fake swordplay with Yoda, who doubled as Captain Hook.

For a while, Mei even forgot about the strain, the struggle to say all the right words since he'd returned. It was so simple to make her daughter laugh, to appreciate Travis's own belly-deep chuckles as he caused Isabel to applaud at the end of the impromptu performance.

Mei even found *herself* laughing again, and it felt so good. Cleansing and right.

The easiness even continued after they left Isabel slumbering in her plush-crowded bed.

Walking down the hall together, they headed for the family room. Just as they were about to enter, Travis took Mei's hand, then gently pulled her along with him to the couch.

"What a day," he said, the low lighting giving the area a quiet, anticipatory glow as they sat.

He smiled and hooked an arm around her shoulders, drawing her closer, and it was all Mei could do to contain a delicious tremble at the slant of his hard chest, the security of his muscled arms.

Lord help her, she was a split second away from giving in to anything he suggested at this point….

A combination of fear and excitement coursed through her, a thread of adrenaline barely holding her together. She inhaled, thinking only about how good he smelled, like a forest morning. There was also a hint of musk from a man who was used to sweating—a clean yet primal base.

He rested his mouth against her head and murmured, "I've missed you like crazy."

Her pulse thrashed. "Tell me about it."

But Travis wasn't finished. He lowered his persuasive tone even more, drawing her back in until she was flailing inside.

"What comes next, Mei?" he asked.

Another kiss, she thought, craving it.

Then she thought of a second "next." The possibility of another child.

Were they on strong-enough footing yet? Could she tell him? After all, this was the man who had known exactly how Mei felt at the restaurant when Li had reminded her of the neurotic need to always please her family. And who else could've comforted Mei so genuinely?

They had so much history, so much to fight for....

Travis seemed to understand her hesitation. "When you're ready, I'm going to be there. I'm not going to push you."

"Okay." Relief overran the anxiety in her veins. Yet it didn't cancel out the still-pumping excitement of just sitting next to him, feeling the overwhelming heat of his body so near hers.

"I mean," she said, "it takes a lot of pressure off. And it's not that I don't want to…"

She trailed off, afraid to say anything more, mostly because she wasn't sure if she could take it.

"Want to what?" he asked, his breathing uneven.

She looked him straight in the eye. "It's not that I don't want to be with you again. Because I do, and I can barely manage to keep a level head when you're this close."

His gaze blazed—waves of appetite rumbling and growing.

Coating her dry throat, she swallowed. "Sex would cloud the issues."

"Yes, it would. It's clouding them right now."

His forthrightness, his willpower, his vow to make

things right touched her. So did his support back at the restaurant; it had made her realize that she'd never lost that from him, even when so much else had waned.

She'd never stopped loving this man at all, and that was everything.

Steadying her pulse, she got up from the couch, knowing what *did* need to happen next, even before they made love again. "I'm going to de-cloud things for a minute, okay?"

He ran a hand through his dark hair. "You're right. You're absolutely right. But," he added hopefully, "you'll come back to watch a movie on TV?" He raised his hands again, all innocence. "I promise—I'll be a saint."

Mei couldn't breathe. He didn't realize that everything would change once she came back out here—that is, if the pregnancy test results revealed what she suspected they might.

"I'll be back soon." She smiled, even though she was all nerves inside, then headed for her bathroom. The cabinet.

The test.

Surely we've come far enough, she thought. *We still have so much to build on, and if I do end up being pregnant, it'll be good news, not another source for worry....*

Locking both the bedroom and bathroom doors behind her, she opened her private drawer, her hands shaking as she fumbled with the test's box. Maybe she should wait to take it in the morning, when the results might be more effective, but she'd waited too long already.

A minute later, she was watching the stick.

Please, she thought, realizing just how badly she did

want another child with him. It was all she'd desired for so long, all she'd dreamed of.

And when the readout showed a smiley face, her heart almost shot out of her chest.

Her vision blurred, and she was consumed by such happiness that she could hardly stand. After slipping the stick into the plastic sheath it'd come in, she washed up, then unlocked the bathroom door, her pulse kicking at her chest.

He would be happy, too, Mei told herself. Travis wanted to be a part of the family again, and this would be a surprising welcome home.

Wouldn't it...?

When the old doubts attempted to butt their way in to her pep talk, Mei forced them away. She wouldn't think about what might happen if he fell right back in to volunteering too much and neglecting his duties at home.

Wouldn't think about that at all.

She held the stick behind her back as she opened her bedroom door and went to the family room, where her husband was channel surfing.

Blue light from the screen suffused his strong, handsome face.

Would their second child look like Isabel, a mix of both Travis and Mei? Or would this baby look more like him?

At the notion, her stomach tumbled, just as if the life inside were rolling in celebration. Mei placed a hand there, joining in the sublime glee.

We're all going to be happy once your daddy and I get everything settled....

She got closer. "Travis? I—"

She stopped when she realized that he wasn't switching channels any longer, that the TV screen was now glowing orange with an image that had transfixed him.

A newscast of a fire across the country.

His posture was stiff, almost as if he were ready to jump up from the couch. She could see his jaw clenching, his eyes staring intently....

Yearningly?

Her grip loosened on the stick hidden behind her back, and it fell out of her hand, smacking to the floor.

While watching the screen, Travis didn't see the flames at all.

No, he'd seen the nightmares, the hand reaching out to him.

The hand he could never quite grasp.

But then he had a delayed reaction, finally responding to the voice he'd thought he'd heard behind him a few seconds ago.

He turned, finding Mei, her lips parted, her eyes burnished with pink smudges.

When he stood, she flinched and bent down to retrieve something she'd dropped. Whatever it was, she stuffed it into her skirt pocket.

"Mei?" he asked, feeling guilty for getting sucked into his obsessions again, even if it'd just been on the TV. Feeling even more remorseful that his instinct was to shut her out of it.

After snapping the TV off with the remote, he tossed the device on the couch, taking his self-disgust out on himself with the gesture. "It was in Texas," he said, referring to the fire. "And if you're thinking that I'm packing up to go there—"

She shook her head, as if to deny the sheer possibility. "You wouldn't."

Was she trying to convince herself of that?

He approached slowly, scanning her reddened eyes. "I make you so sad. Even now, when I've been trying so hard not to."

She placed her hand on her pocket for the briefest instant, then folded her arms over her stomach. "I just hate to see you tortured, Travis. The way you were watching that screen. I wish I knew how to make that end."

End?

For some reason, the comment made him feel as if something had slipped out of his clutches—or near-clutches. Good God, if he let go of this mission of his, would it be tantamount to turning his back on that nightmarish hand?

Because that's what he was doing every time he went on shift—making sense out of death. Trying to erase it, cheat it, by stealing another soul away from the destruction.

"You're never going to stop," Mei said as if her heart were cracking. "You might cut back on hours and be home with us, but you're never really going to *be* here, are you?"

He sank into a chair, wishing he had the power to go on with life as his siblings had done after their mom's death. Even his dad had gotten over it, but then again, none of them had the physical means to help others the way Travis could.

It was his duty to stop it from happening again. His calling.

Wasn't it?

"Mom was the one who started to accept our marriage," he said, staring straight ahead. "She was coming around. She loved Isabel and was a good grandmother, and she renewed my faith in her once that happened. Then all of a sudden…"

"She was gone." Mei spread out her hands but didn't say anything, as if there were no adequate words anymore.

"You know," he added, feeling so empty in the face of this setback, "she used to always be on my side when Dad got on my case about not putting my toy trucks back in their exact spot in the garage. Or when Dad dressed me down about the B-plus I'd gotten on an essay instead of an A. She was always there to open my bedroom door, sit on my bed and assure me that I was still loved. That it wasn't the end of the world."

Mei still remained across the room, but her soft, warm scent brushed over him. Into him.

"When I started seeing you," he said, "that was the only time she got somewhat standoffish, but that was because she had her heart set on me marrying someone in our social set."

"Which you never felt comfortable with, anyway."

"And she came around to knowing that." His mom. His champion. "And when she left, things weren't the same. Especially with Dad."

"Travis," Mei hugged herself tighter. "You can't bring her back. She's never going to be the bridge between you and your father again."

He was startled at the depth of Mei's understanding. This was another reason he was fighting so hard—so he could bring back the one person who'd made him feel close to his dad.

Right?

So he could bring her back and make his family happy and be the son he'd always attempted to be?

Mei reached out, even from the distance that separated them. He saw it as a last chance, another offer of help. But he wanted to protect her from everything, just as he protected the community.

Was he trying to save her from himself by closing her off?

While all this was going through his head, she must have interpreted his hesitation as denial, and she lowered her hand to her side.

Why? she seemed to be asking. *Are you so comfortable with these patterns that you really* can't *change?*

Won't change?

He wanted to tell Mei that he hadn't rejected *her,* just all the rest of it, but she was already walking toward her room.

"Stay," he said. "Just a little longer. Tell me what you were going to say earlier?"

She paused at the hallway, her hand resting against the wall. It was shaking.

Then as if coming to some sort of decision, she whispered, "I wasn't going to say anything." Then she started toward her bedroom once again.

Chapter Eight

Mei never actually went to bed.

Her mind wouldn't settle, not after this latest setback with Travis, so she took out a cozy mystery—something amusing about a cat helping an amateur detective solve a crime—and hoped her eyes would start to close. Reading was usually a good relaxant.

But this time, it didn't work. That's why, at around midnight, she finally got out of bed, taking the mystery with her. She intended to read it on the couch in front of a murmuring TV for company.

Yet that ended up not being very appealing, so she ransacked the fridge instead, popped a few grapes into her mouth, then decided that her stomach couldn't handle any more food.

She sought other options to quell her restlessness,

thinking about getting out some knitting she'd stuffed in a box in her closet, but…nah. Then there was her computer; she could go online. But that was in the guest room, where Travis was staying, so, needless to say, it wasn't a choice.

Not with the way she was wrestling the urge to knock on his door to see if he was awake for reasons other than using the computer.

She realized she was absently walking back and forth in the family room and halted her steps, cradling her belly with one arm.

No matter what had happened between them, they were going to have another baby. *A baby.*

Although she'd tried hard to hide how crushed she'd been by seeing how he missed being on the job, she wished she could share her personal joy with him. Even if she could just quietly cuddle up against him as he held her, feeling his body against hers in the absolute miracle of what should've been good fortune.

To make things more acute, in the past when she couldn't sleep, she would always sidle up next to Travis in bed. She didn't even have that now.

Dropping her book on the couch, Mei gripped the back of the furniture, as if that could anchor her from straying into the hallway and giving in to her primal, hormonal cravings.

This was lonely. How could she feel so isolated from him when he was so close?

When *they* had been so close to improving?

But she was still uncomfortable with letting him in on the news, when they were already dealing with so much else.

Then again, what *would* be so wrong about silently touching him now and explaining the emotion behind it later?

She could just rest easy in his arms with the knowledge that things would improve, that her loneliness would subside with him around. Or maybe his embrace could make her believe they would get to the point where she could tell him about baby number two in a moment of pure love for each other, uninterrupted by all this stress and worry.

He's just down the hall, Mei, she thought. *That's all the distance you need to travel to be close to him tonight, to do a little more mending for the future.*

She clutched the couch for a moment longer, until the poignant craving to go to him subsided. Then, after telling herself to try that cozy mystery again in her bed, she forced herself to retreat to her room.

Yet her best intentions blew up in her face only a moment after she'd entered. Duh. She'd dropped her book on the couch and needed to go back to get it.

However, she didn't even get past the doorway, where she found Travis standing, ruffling his fingers through his dark, sleep-mussed hair.

He wore only long pale blue pajama bottoms that left his torso bare, exposing broad shoulders and a muscle-hewn chest, thick arms, ridged abs.

Her heart jammed in her throat, flittering like a butterfly escaping from a pair of closed hands. She clasped her arms over her chest, covering the shadowed vulnerability of her long white linen nightgown.

"Thought I heard you up and about," he said, low voice vibrating over her skin.

The blood that she'd tried to keep lukewarm boiled until it slid through her, settling between her legs in a sharp ache.

We made another baby, she thought, needing him tonight. Needing him to know that she really did wish to share the news, even though they had so much more to conquer before she could.

Standing here, feet away from him…

Lonely. So lonely for the husband she wanted to love.

In an act of willpower, she glanced away from his gorgeous body and focused on his eyes. They were narrowed, no doubt because he'd gone from the darkness of the hallway to the light from her room.

"You can't sleep, either?" he whispered, minding that Isabel's room was down the hall.

She did the same. "Not really. Sorry for rattling around out there. I tried not to make a lot of noise."

"You were as quiet as a mouse. It's just that I was hearing *everything*—a car going by outside, voices from a couple of people on the sidewalk who had a late night out. I could even hear the air going by."

Keep looking at his eyes, she thought, even though his gaze was just as tempting as his bared chest. She couldn't win.

"Seems as if we've both been having insomnia lately," she said.

"Imagine that."

They just stood there, inches into her bedroom, a place where they'd shared so much only a month ago: the same bathroom while getting ready for their different daily schedules. The same bed where they had last made love.

He shrugged. "I decided to poke around in my e-mail to pass the time. If you want to check yours…"

"That's all right."

Why did they sound so darn polite with each other? As if he really *was* a visitor staying in the guest room?

You're having his baby. You already have a beautiful child together….

Couldn't she just go to him now, press against his naked skin? Was it so wrong to reassure herself for even a short time that Travis would be here?

There was a cherrywood vanity table near the door, a piece that they had purchased long ago at the beginning of their marriage. It also kept her ring secure in its long drawer.

He angled toward the furniture and traced a finger over one of the perfume bottles she kept on a mirrored tray. It was almost as if he were caressing her, and her flesh responded by flushing.

"I got an e-mail from Carrie," he said, voice quietly shattering the still of the night.

Carrie, his older sister.

Mei got the feeling he'd come out of his room when he'd heard her because he wanted to talk about this e-mail. "How is she?"

"Great. The kids are back in school and they're all plotting a trip to Orlando during winter break."

"Sounds fun." She remembered planning for future trips once upon a time, too.

"Carrie also mentioned something about my dad."

Here it was. "Is he okay?"

"Sure. Yeah." Travis had stopped touching the perfume bottle and was just staring at it. "I mean, he took a fall down a couple of stairs for some reason. Not a bad one, but… Damn, he's not even that old."

"Fifty-five, right?"

"Uh-huh. The doctor said it's because of that old tennis injury. His hip."

"Are you…" She moved nearer to her husband. "Are you thinking about seeing him? Just to make sure he's okay?"

Travis tensed. "He doesn't need my second opinion. I've got 'paramedic' in my job title, but it wouldn't occur to him that I'm more than the son who turned my white collar blue."

Now Mei was at the vanity table, too, and she could see the dimmed image of her and Travis in the upright mirror. All the physical—and mental—space between them was reflected back like a distant judgment.

But looking away from the mirror, she found that she was only a reach away from him.

Her head swam. Pheromones, she thought. He invaded her with his musky scent, the thick heat of his proximity.

"I think," she said softly, "Carrie's hinting that you should see your dad."

"She's always hinting that."

"He *is* getting older, Travis. Maybe this is his way of finally approaching you, even though it's through your sister."

He reached for another bottle of perfume, an older one that she'd kept more out of sentimentality than usefulness. An orange blossom fragrance that had probably surrendered all its scent over time. Travis used to love it, but the manufacturer had discontinued the product.

He smiled as he caressed the etched glass, and her

pulse banged like a drum echoing in a room that was just starting to fill up with people. In spite of herself, Mei closed her eyes because he was so close she could feel his skin on hers, even from a slight distance away.

When she opened her eyes, she discovered him watching her, his gaze heated.

Her heartbeat pounded at her temples, shredding up every rational thought. The lining of her belly trembled, and once again, she brushed a hand over it.

Good heavens, she wanted to share the news in the only way she could right now.

Instinct goaded her to cover his hand, which still lingered on the second perfume bottle. At the contact, everything that had been holding her back imploded, sucking in to her with a pain that doubled as pleasure.

So much denied pleasure.

His skin, so rough, so familiar, burned at the touch, as if it were giving off sparks that needled her nerve endings. Electricity shot beneath her skin, charring her, making her ache.

"Mei, do you know what you're doing?" His tone sounded battered.

She nodded, even though she realized this wouldn't solve anything. She'd spent a lot of time resisting his charm and determination in order to convince herself that his affection was real, but she was beyond that now.

With a shaking exhalation, she turned over his hand, ran her fingers over his roughened palm and up the inside of his arm where veins textured the thinner skin.

"It's time for us to move on," she murmured, remembering how he'd watched that fire.

And maybe doing anything she could to vanquish it. "But…"

She understood his confusion, yet she would explain later, when they had worked up to being ready for this latest twist in their relationship. Presently, all she wanted was flesh, warmth, comfort.

Whether it was right or wrong.

When she tenderly skimmed the tips of her fingers into the crook of his arm, he jerked at the stimulation.

"I just don't want you to regret anything, Mei." His Adam's apple worked in his throat as he swallowed.

We're having a baby….

She closed the rest of the distance between them, her nightgown whisking against his torso as she peered up into his gaze.

"I won't regret it if you give me no reason to," she said. "You know I won't."

A flash of him sitting there and watching the TV fire stabbed her before she shoved it away, concentrating instead on a throbbing vein in his neck. She could almost hear the echo of it in her own heart, and the cacophony soon overtook every passing moment.

Never disconnecting from his gaze, she reached for the bedroom door, pushed it shut. When she came back to him, he welcomed her by slipping his hands underneath her jawline, his thumbs brushing her cheeks.

They looked at each other—so in love, so afraid it would leave them.

As he lowered his lips to hers, she closed her eyes. Then, at the touch of his mouth—wet, warm, soft—her vision wavered, rolling like a tattered flag in the wind.

Her body took up the motion, too, undulating, flowing in and out of itself with liquid ecstasy.

She parted her lips, leaning into his hard body until her breasts crushed against him, then wincing when he accepted her invitation and slid his tongue inside her mouth.

The kiss intensified, raw and erotic, with him exploring her. With her inviting him farther.

Deeper. Longer.

Passion washed through Mei, and the ache between her legs pierced until she pressed against his growing arousal. Even with his pajama bottoms and her nightgown, the prodding stiffness gave her a certain amount of relief—and breathless anguish—as she parted her legs and urged him on.

He responded by clasping her in an embrace, then disengaging from the kiss with a heaving inhalation and burying his face in her loose hair.

"I've imagined this so many times in the past month," he said.

Joy rushed her. It was evidence that she was still a big part of him, owning the section of his mind that wasn't given over to revenge. Hearing him voice it was a balm, another reason to celebrate.

Mei ran her hands over his skin, his well-worked muscles. Panting against him, she reveled in the humidity of their contact, her nightgown beginning to stick to her flesh.

Tenderly, he backed away just enough to gaze into her eyes, to whip her body back into a frenzy again with his silent, intense promise of a true reunion.

He grasped her nightgown, then started to slide it up,

over her skin, the linen teasing her as it brushed her stomach, her already-distended nipples.

She lifted her arms while he worked the material all the way off, then tossed it to the floor. But before she could put her arms back down, he caught them, keeping them over her head and running a famished gaze over her.

"Oh, babe," he said, breath quickening even more.

Resting one of his hands on her collarbone, he then sketched downward: between the breasts that were only slightly fuller than when he'd left, down the center of her stomach, down to her belly.

He paused there, and Mei's tummy somersaulted.

It was almost as if he knew….

The fantasy goaded her, blocking every last bit of common sense altogether.

Travis. All there was right now was him, *them*.

Affectionately, he rubbed his knuckles over her belly, making her throb and grow even moister. No turning back.

Too far gone…

Propping her arms on her head, she moved with his motions. "Yes," she whispered.

"Not yet, Mei. After all this time away from you, I want to make this last."

Why did it sound as if he were talking about more than this encounter?

"I don't know how long I *can* last," she murmured.

He pressed his mouth against her forehead. "Okay, me, neither."

Then he coaxed his fingers into her lace panties, and she grabbed his shoulders, her knees almost buckling.

She thought she heard him laugh—a contented sound that made her think all he wanted to do was please her.

And he went on to prove that theory as he guided her toward the bed, laying her on the tangled sheets, carefully, using one hand to spread her hair out so it wouldn't get caught under her.

His actions were so deliberate, so aware of what she needed, that her heart swelled.

But even as she thought she'd banished every doubt, that voice of reason barged to the front of her consciousness, getting in one last whisper.

How long will this last?

She cuffed it away and shifted her hips as her husband tugged down her panties. The air hit her when he eased open her legs.

Exposed, she waited as he shucked off his pajama bottoms, revealing his arousal. As he came to her again, she couldn't take her eyes off of him, not even after he kneeled between her bent knees.

Now she was plumped and pounding, so ready for him. Her body felt pummeled by the heightened emotion of keeping the secret from him, of wanting so badly to tell him when she shouldn't.

He leaned forward, hungry, prowling, then smoothed his hands up her torso until he cupped her breasts.

As he kneaded them, she squirmed, loving the slightly increased sensitivity. And when he took one, then the other, in his mouth, she wrapped a leg around him, insisting he come nearer.

Come *in* to her.

But he was taking his time instead, as if reacquainting himself with every inch of her. He sucked at her breasts, laved at them, coasted his tongue high and low until she strained against him.

"Travis…" she said, fisting his hair in her hands.

Yet he only smiled, then trailed his lips downward, pushing her legs wider until his tongue found her most private spot.

She bit back a cry as he kissed her there, then loved her with a passion so thorough that every part of her sang with high-strung tension.

And just when she came to the edge, tilting over it, losing her equilibrium, he covered her with his body, entering her with one long, slick plunge.

Mei groaned, careful not to be too loud, but needing the release all the same. She clung to him, Travis, husband, hero, and vowed she would tell him soon.

Soon.

Her emotions threatened to get away from her, but she was still mindful of their baby's comfort, so she maneuvered so that she was on top of him.

Soaring, driving…

Bringing him to a climax that burst into her with a searing blossom of heat.

Then, taking her by the hips, he helped churn Mei to her own orgasm. She leaned back, gyrating, reaching, even though she wasn't sure what was just beyond her grasp except for pure sublimity.

Unbalanced, she wavered, losing it, not sure about anything…

Then her mind, her vision, went star-spangled black—

She stiffened, falling over that edge, reality tilting.

Then, as she flailed to grip something, a flash of color assaulted her, and she changed direction, hitting a rainbowed wall with an exploding riot of flame.

It was only afterward, as she sank to Travis and rested her head on his chest, that she heard his heartbeat go slow and calm, just as hers was doing.

Gently, she took his hand and placed it on her belly, doing her best to let him in on the secret.

Yet keeping it secure just for the time being.

As they lay there, the room's soft light covering them like a light blanket, Travis hugged Mei to his sweat-coated chest. Her black hair stuck to his skin in long, smooth waves, and her hand covered his as he held it to her belly in the waning afterglow.

She'd opened herself to him, and it had been beyond his power to resist or question just why she'd changed her mind.

But, dammit, they were married. Their desire for each other had been natural. Why couldn't he just accept their making love as the next step toward a better marriage?

Or should he just be enjoying his good fortune and hoping it lasted?

Quite innocently, she brushed her fingers over his ribs, and his need for her coiled in his belly yet again.

"You're not going to regret what just happened," he said, teasing, testing. "Are you?"

She rested her lips near his nipple, one leg thrown over his own. His arousal stirred that much more.

"No." She sighed against him, snuggling. "I'm happy. Happier than I've been in a long time."

"But…" He stopped himself, then decided he was just going to be honest. "I thought, earlier tonight, with the fire on the TV… You seemed withdrawn."

She paused. "You were so great at Li's restaurant. I…lost my head. I suppose I was even swept away." Then, as if she didn't want to talk about it anymore, she teasingly said, "You're not complaining, are you?"

"Hardly."

He still didn't understand, but maybe things *had* improved.

Had they been wrong about sex not solving anything?

He pushed back the hair that was hiding her face. At the sight of her dainty features, he constricted, wanting her—loving her.

His Mei. Tonight had only made that all the clearer.

"Remember when you said we need to have more than just passion for each other?" he asked.

"Vividly."

He smiled. "Well, it's also about spending more than time together. You're in my heart, Mei, whether we're sitting in front of TV with Isabel or alone and making love."

She held to him tighter, as if something was pulling at her. "Travis."

Her overly emotional tone of voice struck him.

Then she rested her face against him, and he folded both arms over her.

"I suppose," she continued, her lips against his skin, "in the back of my mind, I wondered if the first time we had sex again would be hurtful. If our differences would come out in bed. But they didn't."

He leaned his cheek against her head. No words could describe what he'd actually experienced: a renewal, a cleansing at having been inside of her. Making love had been different this time because he was keenly aware of what he'd almost forfeited.

Yet the fact remained—he still had to let *her* inside in a much more intimate, scarier way.

"But," she added, "we both know that our affection for each other isn't the issue. We'll have to be patient because we're not going to fix everything in a few days or even a few weeks."

"We're on our way."

She pushed up from him, watching him with what seemed to be her bruised heart in her eyes.

"Yes," she said. "We're on our way."

Why did she still carry a hint of sadness, then?

Travis wouldn't accept it. "You know what I'm gonna do now?"

An easy step compared to what he really should do—let go of his anger. Let her help.

"What?" she whispered.

He wrapped a strand of her hair around his finger, then watched it uncurl back into rainfall straightness. "All this family tension. We don't need it. So after Cousin Li mentioned that birthday party tomorrow night, I decided I'd go."

Mei's eyes seemed to light up a little. "Really?"

"Hey, I made it through Li tonight, didn't I?"

"Yes, but…" She paused. "I don't expect you to bust into the lion's den right now, Travis. They're still wondering why you were gone for so long and they don't quite understand. Don't get me wrong, because you know they appreciate that someone's out there protecting them, but—"

"They just don't want it to be your husband."

"They're concerned for you…and me and Isabel, too." Mei smiled and laid her head on her pillow, her eyes heavy-lidded. Sleepy. "Just like I'm afraid for you when you're out there taking extra risks."

He touched her cheek, wishing he could loosen his grip on fighting and hold *her* even closer instead.

But when it came right down to it, he was afraid, wasn't he? Frightened of what she might think if she saw how dark it really was in his mind, how hopeless sometimes.

"You don't have to go to that party," she repeated. "Sincerely."

"I want to. I—"

He cut himself off when she closed her eyes, a tiny smile on her mouth.

After watching her, then tucking a strand of damp hair behind her ear, Travis sat up, turned out the light and settled back down into the bed.

He was giving her his time, but not all of his soul, he thought.

And until he could bring himself to expose all his fears, his weakness to her, this marriage would always be in trouble.

Chapter Nine

The designated birthday party house was a short drive to Novato, and they arrived there a half hour before sweet-sixteen-year-old Natalie was to be surprised by all the extended Chang family in the area.

When Travis first walked into the two-level stucco-and-brick house, he had his defenses up and running. In fact, he could detect the judgments going on behind the smiling faces.

Sure, they were nice to him. It was just that they were *too* nice, and he'd always felt more like a guest than a part of the clan.

But he'd spent a lot of time earning this subtle treatment. Besides, how often had he gone to one of their soirees, anyway? In spite of all the energy he'd put into learning about Mei's life back when they'd first fallen in love, he wasn't sure he was now acquainted with a lot of the family well enough to be more than a visitor.

They all gathered in the large common room, with its lacquered cabinets and chests, plus rosewood love seats and oil paintings depicting Victoria Harbour and its Hong Kong skyline. However, the main attraction seemed to be a table laden with the food every guest had brought.

After Travis, Mei and Isabel greeted many of the others, including Mei's maternal and paternal grandparents in addition to her three brothers, they took Isabel to an adjacent room where she immediately began playing Candy Land with kids of her own age while Mei and Travis gravitated toward the buffet.

There, they rested in a corner, smiling at everyone who came to get food.

"When's the birthday girl due to walk through the door?" asked Uncle Kenneth as he walked past them, piling a paper plate high with roasted duck. He was the relative who had sponsored Mei and her family in coming to this country—a man with permanent laugh lines surrounding his mouth and eyes, his hair a metallic gray.

His wife, Aunt Stephanie, dragged him away from the table when he began to eye the buttercream frosted birthday cake. Besides having a store of good humor, Uncle Kenneth also boasted a notoriously uncontrollable sweet tooth.

"Natalie had cheerleading practice," she reminded her husband. "She'll be here anytime."

"Practice, my foot," he said as he took position near Travis. Kenneth winked at Mei. "I'll bet our cheerleader is making eyes at the football team instead. That's what's slowing her down."

Everyone laughed, the ice broken. Kenneth reached out his free hand to shake Travis's. "Glad you could come." Uncle Kenneth then moved on to welcome Mei.

Aunt Stephanie, a petite woman with short black hair and sparkling brown eyes, did the same as she addressed a comment to her niece. "I don't see your parents here."

"Dad was at the optometrist and Mom was driving him," she answered. "They called to tell me that the doctor was running late."

"Doctors around here." Aunt Stephanie shook her head. "All these HMOs…"

As if to avoid this topic, Uncle Kenneth turned to Travis. "I didn't think they ever gave you danger boys a night off."

Travis had been wondering if he could avoid his job for even an hour or two. Apparently not. "I've got a few more days of vacation left."

Mei wasn't far behind with the explanations. "He's been taking us on picnics and working on projects around the house."

She slipped her hand into his, and her aunt and uncle both showed approving expressions.

Was she taking up his cause? Or was she just on the defensive with her family?

Travis wasn't quite sure, even though today had been a good one. While Isabel was at school, he and Mei had worked on their own business at home—she sewing up a slew of baby blankets and he bolting some new shelves for the family room on the walls; he didn't get to all of them, but he would take care of that later. However, every time they passed in the hallway or in the common space, they would touch each other's arms, shoulders, faces—soft, sensual, tentative tributes to last night that he hoped would continue.

"Things have finally started to settle down since Isabel was born," Mei said, clearly diverting the subject away from Travis's job, which he appreciated.

"And where is the sweetheart?" Stephanie asked.

"Next room, with the other little ones," Mei said.

Unlike Stephanie, Kenneth didn't turn to look in that direction. "I imagine that some of the craziness around your home has to do with that business you started. The Internet site for the babies."

Now it was Travis's turn to back up Mei. He knew that business could be a sore spot with her and Uncle Kenneth, seeing as she had turned down a job with his furniture-importing company in favor of going with Webb Incorporated.

"Baby Boom-Boom," he said proudly, glancing at Mei and smiling.

"Sales are growing," she said, seeming proud, too.

Had she brought up this topic so she could remind Kenneth that she had done well for herself on her own?

She continued. "The business is a small venture so far, but that's how most of them start out, right?"

Aunt Stephanie had trained her gaze on the food table, as if removing herself from the discussion.

"True," Kenneth said. "But if you need anything, you let me know."

For some reason, Travis felt as if the older man wasn't appreciating what Mei had accomplished, although he wasn't being unkind about it.

Couldn't he acknowledge that she was a mother who held down the home front *and* a business on her own?

When Mei went quiet, he knew her thoughts echoed his own.

Travis was hardly bristling, but he was determined to make a point. "Your support means a lot, Kenneth, but Mei's being real modest. A couple months ago, she found a few ways to capitalize on inexpensive advertising by networking with playgroups online. Her profit margin has doubled since then."

She'd told him this once when he'd been home between volunteer shifts. But he'd remembered, even during his hectic pursuits.

Mei lowered her gaze to the ground and squeezed his hand at the same time, obviously thanking him for his defense of her.

And maybe even appreciating that he *had* remembered.

"But," Mei added, "as Travis said, we appreciate the support. It means a lot, Uncle Kenneth."

By this time, Aunt Stephanie had tuned back in to the conversation, and she was beaming at Mei, as if impressed with her niece, too.

Uncle Kenneth chuckled and toasted them with his plate, but Travis could tell he was a man who wasn't used to having his offers turned down. He'd been in this country for a long time, though—his parents were even born here, and he often told everyone that he had a one-hundred-percent-American attitude, although he definitely had old-school qualities about him, as well.

Actually, Travis suspected he also admired Mei's drive and ambition.

"Just look at this husband of yours," Uncle Kenneth said to his niece. "He's a valuable PR asset."

Without even glancing, Travis felt Mei's gaze on him. The warmth transcended words.

"Mei amazes me every new day." He held her hand to his heart. "The way she sets her mind on a goal and accomplishes it. The way she handles every moment with such grace and beauty. How can I not love everything about her?"

Mei's dark eyes had grown wider and softer, and everything else around them—the crowd, the room—ceased to exist. There was only the two of them, a couple once again. A team.

Someone cleared his throat, and the moment broke open with the jarring reintroduction of voices rising in discussions.

Then, before Travis could gauge Kenneth's and Stephanie's reactions to his declaration, the lights flickered as someone jiggled a switch. Afterward, the room buzzed to silence when the birthday girl's mother announced that Natalie had just pulled up in the driveway with the high school boyfriend who had been tasked with getting her to the party.

At that point, the children from the next room bolted from their games and rejoined their parents. Isabel was so out of breath and excited about yelling "Happy Birthday!" to her cousin that she didn't even notice how Mei was lavishing a long, hope-filled gaze on Travis.

"Birthday, birthday…!" she kept saying, hopping up and down after grabbing Travis's free hand.

He held his daughter, putting an arm around Mei, too. They felt so much better than any crusade.

Everyone else settled to a hush, facing the entrance to the living room. Then, as the birthday girl came through the door, the crowd belted, "Surprise!"

They all launched into the birthday song, followed by post-melody applause.

Heart in his throat, Travis watched Mei clapping and smiling, drawn to her good heart, her glow.

Even after all he'd done, he still thought there was more he could do to show her the level of his commitment. Dammit, if he could shout his love from the rooftops he'd sure as hell do it.

But it also occurred to him that maybe he was looking for a way to edge around that ultimate sacrifice he should be making instead....

He skirted around that and set his mind to what would make Mei feel like the most important woman in the world.

The night wore on, with another aunt and another cousin and others eventually claiming Mei's attention. But that only gave Travis the opportunity to refine this idea of his.

This desperate act of winning her back because he couldn't manage anything more without falling apart himself.

After the birthday girl, who was still dressed in a practice cheer skirt and a top announcing "Rebels," blew out the candles, Mei's parents arrived.

She first spotted them across the room exchanging pleasantries with Travis, who had left Mei earlier to socialize with relatives.

Mei wasn't certain if he was trying to impress her or what, but when she saw him being so attentive to her dad and mom, she decided it didn't matter.

And, weirdly, her parents somehow seemed open to whatever he was discussing with them.

Yes, *open*.

Wondering what could possibly have brought this about, she kept tabs on the situation while sitting on the floor with Isabel and a few of the other children who had crowded round to hear the entertaining stories she often told at these gatherings. It'd gotten to the point where, at some moment during each social event, she was the go-to girl for at least fifteen minutes of entertainment between hide-and-go-seek and eating.

Without quite realizing it, she had stopped in the telling of the story of the Foolish Old Man Who Moved a Mountain.

Richie, one of her nephews, yanked on Mei's skirt, which had belled out around her as she sat.

"Auntie?" he asked.

Mei dragged her gaze away from Travis just as he left her parents and sauntered to the food table for his plate of cake. Her dad and mom traded raised eyebrows, then were set upon by some third cousins.

Turning back to the children, Mei smiled. "Sorry about that. Where was I?"

The question was more of a tease than anything, and Richie's voice rang over the others.

"The Wise Old Man at the River Bend tells the Foolish Old Man it's dumb to move a mountain."

"Ah, right." She started where she'd left off, but her mind was hardly on the telling.

Her mind—her *emotions*—had been in a swirling haze all night. How could they not be while this new, wonderful Travis was doing his best to fit in with her relatives?

And how could she forget how he'd championed her with Uncle Kenneth?

Now all the children were staring, their heads tilted.

Mei waved a hand in front of her face, feeling flushed. "Let's leave the rest of the story for our potluck at the end of the month."

Some of the children groaned, but Mei sent them a sweet grin. They knew she would remember them come the next gathering.

By the time she stood, Travis had been cornered by Cousin Li's teenage son, Tommy, and also Natalie's boyfriend, Sage. The young men were no doubt milking firefighting tales out of her husband, and Mei decided not to measure how much enjoyment Travis might be getting out of reliving the job.

Not when things had been going so well tonight.

Even so, thoughts of how he'd looked in front of the TV, when he'd watched that fire burn, got to her, and she shut them out, going to the beverage bowl to pour herself another plastic glass of citrus-laced punch.

"There she is," said her father from behind her. He spoke Chinese. "Our wonderful daughter."

Mei faced them—Dad with his thick, black-framed glasses and balding hair. Mom with her pearl necklace and powder-blue Jackie O. suit.

She hugged both of them, but braced herself for any impending comments about Travis. Sure, her parents always made subtle, veiled chastisements about the choices Mei had made in life, but to her they could sound like announcements filling every corner of the room.

Yet her parents surprised her this time.

"Where is Isabel?" Mom asked. "It feels as if I haven't seen her in weeks."

"She's somewhere around here, and didn't you just have her overnight?"

Her dad laughed. "A grandmother's job is never done."

A pause. Then Mei asked if they would like punch, and she poured two glasses of the beverage. Another pause. She was just waiting for them to comment on Travis being here.

Yet…nope.

Finally, she couldn't stand it anymore. "You already saw Travis?"

"Yes." Her father took a sip of punch. "He welcomed us to the party, as a matter of fact. Very kind of him."

Her mom nodded and smiled.

Okay, so they didn't have all that much to say. Seriously strange.

And when they started talking about the eye doctor and how her father should switch, Mei's weird meter started going nuts.

She followed the topic to its end, then went for it.

"So you're not shocked to see him here? You seemed to be having a good conversation…?"

"Yes, we were," her dad said vaguely.

But her mom had more to say—at least if you counted up her words, came up with a total and then ignored the content altogether. "It's certainly a nice surprise to see him, and…"

She seemed about to say something more, but her dad put a gentle hand on her mom's arm.

"A surprise indeed," he said.

Her parents traded cryptic looks.

Mei almost pursued it, but her mother scoped the room and found Isabel, then announced that she wanted to say hello to her granddaughter.

She bustled off, but her dad lingered behind for a moment, looking at Mei—really looking at her—then smiled and nodded before following his wife across the room.

What had *that* been about?

More important, what had Travis said to her parents?

She glanced where she'd last seen him, but he wasn't there. Nonetheless, she headed for the corner where he'd been standing with Tommy and Sage. The two teens were still around, eating their cake and talking through the crumbs.

When Mei asked where her husband had gone, the boys stood a little straighter. It gave Mei a measure of pride because she knew Travis had that sort of heroic sway over a lot of people.

The teens didn't know where he'd gone, but before Mei could do a search, her brother, Gary, Natalie's father, intercepted her and engaged her in conversation.

All the while, Mei's need to be with Travis burned all the brighter.

And stronger.

* * *

Another hour passed before Mei finally did find Travis.

But it was only after Natalie had finished opening her presents and Isabel had parted from her grandparents to go off somewhere with her father.

"I saw her and Travis heading toward the guest room with all the coats in it," Mom said, while clucking over the new BlackBerry Natalie had received from her parents. The older woman seemed stumped by all its uses.

So Mei headed in the indicated direction, never expecting to find a sight that twisted a hole straight through her chest.

In the night-light-suffused bedroom, she saw coats and purses piled on a bed. In a corner, reclining on a beanbag chair, she found her husband with their daughter lying on his chest, Isabel's small hands balled and her long eyelashes fanned against her cheeks.

His eyes were closed, as well, as if he'd expended all his energy and couldn't summon any more.

The sight of the two of them together, so peaceful, so sweet, tore at Mei, and she held a hand to her own chest, as if feeling the wonderful weight of Isabel there, too. As if trying to keep her heart inside when all it wanted to do was explode outward on its way to zooming right back to Travis.

But all she had to do was place her other hand over her belly, where their second child slept. Then she thought about how Travis had watched that fire on TV....

Yet hadn't he done enough to prove he was on his way to taking care of that?

She bit her bottom lip. Dear Lord, she was so baffled,

but one fact always stood out—he still hadn't reported back to work yet.

His eyes were open now, and he'd obviously been watching her during these pivotal last few seconds. She schooled her expression.

Neutral. Serene.

Then, as if realizing that she'd gone back to her old way of handling things—a way *she* needed to change, too—he whispered, "She's wiped out."

He cradled Isabel's head, a touch so affectionate that Mei's heart melted.

"I'd say someone else is wiped, too," she added.

Travis grinned, but then the gesture disappeared as he looked her up and down.

"Just now, you seemed…" he said, voice soft. "I don't know. Like you were thinking one thing—a really good thing—and then it turned bad."

He tenderly placed a hand over Isabel's exposed ear. "Is it about last night?"

Mei shook her head. He was still concerned about that, and why not? Upon awakening side by side this morning, they hadn't really talked about making love. Maybe that was because he'd been so happy, and she had just wanted the welcome change to last.

But they also hadn't talked about what *tonight* would bring….

"If you're going to ask me if I regret it even after I've had more time to think about it," she said, "the answer is no."

His gaze burned, even in the near dark. "Glad to hear that, because I think the regret gestation period has come and gone."

Gestation.

Their baby.

Touched beyond words, she came to his side and went down on her knees, putting one hand on Isabel's back and the other on his arm. Once again, his scent filled her— man and spice, heady and exhilarating.

"I've been wondering," he whispered, "where I'm going to sleep tonight, Mei, and if it's back in the guest room, so be it. I can take it. I can wait again. Because there will be another time for us. Many more times."

Her body responded with a jolt, infused by recalled fantasies of how his skin had slid along hers, sweat-smooth and friction-tingled. How he had fit into her as if he were a missing element.

At the reminder, she came to nestle against him and their daughter, and the innocence of the moment convinced her that there was no pressure to do anything more. Not now.

As her curves molded to his hard angles, she snuggled further against his neck, keeping her other hand on the slumbering Isabel. A picture of a happy family that would hopefully never fade again.

"Maybe this is enough for tonight?" she asked. "Us holding each other and getting used to being a couple again?"

His hand tightened on her for a moment, but then it loosened, stroking her arm.

He laughed, and she wasn't altogether sure it was because he found anything funny. "If I didn't know any better, I'd say you're enjoying putting me through the paces."

She knew that joking about it was his way of coping. Yet she truly wasn't enjoying any petty revenge.

Not even close.

She was only working on securing him for the long haul, because if she didn't... Well, there'd be no more ultimatums.

Just a crushing finale.

Chapter Ten

Once they got home, the rest of the night went easily—with Mei nested in his arms as they lay in bed, with them slowing things down and concentrating on cuddling so they could be sure their reconciliation wasn't just about the physical.

And, in the morning, all seemed well, even after she'd quizzed him on what he and her parents had been talking about at the party. Her curiosity hadn't abated, and he sure hadn't provided any satisfactory answers.

"They just took it as a positive sign that I came to a gathering," he'd said. "What'd you expect them to do—kick me out?"

Not satisfactory at all, but it was the best she would get.

After rising, Travis and Isabel had run down to the neighborhood market for a big project he'd planned for the day, and while they were gone, Mei made a doctor's appointment for next week, which was the soonest they could see her. Then, when her husband and daughter returned, they all packaged Internet orders for Baby Boom-Boom, with Isabel only doing very light work, of course.

Life was quickly falling into a pattern, wasn't it? Mei thought. She could actually picture Travis working—hopefully at the smaller station—on his twenty-four-hour shift, then coming home for forty-eight hours off to spend quality time with her and their daughter.

For the rest of the day, they all built robots out of old boxes, pipe cleaners and egg cartons, then played something Travis dubbed "Automaton Showdown," which was pretty much a boys-will-be-boys-and-so-will-Travis version of robot wars that made Mei laugh for a couple of hours.

Too good to be true?

Previously, she'd feared that maybe Travis had just been going through the motions, but she felt a real connection between all of them now.

It *had* to last.

The only kink in her day had come when her mother had called, asking her to drop over to their place a few miles away before dinner this evening. Mei hadn't even questioned why since she was always there when asked.

So, while Travis and Isabel ran some cryptic errand that they promised to tell her about later, Mei did her daughterly duty and headed out to a subdivision where the lawns were manicured and the flowers grew over trellises in her parents' condo complex.

Knocking on the door, Mei waited until her mom opened up, then found the older woman dressed to the nines in a pressed burgundy pantsuit that accentuated her small, slender figure.

They hugged, and Mei asked in Chinese, "Special event tonight?"

"Very special."

Mom guided her inside the tiled foyer, with its iron-work candle sconces. Then, linking her arm with Mei's, she brought her to the feng shui-influenced living room, which boasted flower stands, hand-carved architectural pieces and furniture they'd purchased from Uncle Kenneth's showroom.

Her father was sitting on one of the wood-accented couches, dressed in a dark suit, his graying hair combed neatly. They greeted each other, as well.

"Wow," she said. "Is there some sort of church activity you two are attending?"

"Not precisely," Dad said.

Why weren't they saying much?

Something was going on....

Mom had removed herself to the open kitchen, where Mei could see her brewing tea.

"Mei, please do me a favor. I've got something for you in my bedroom. Could you bring it here?"

"What is it?"

"Look on the mattress."

Okay...

Mei climbed the stairs to her parents' bedroom, then entered. When she saw what was waiting on the coverlet of the mattress, she gasped.

It was the red silk dress Mei had worn during the tea ceremony that had taken place just before her church wedding. A beautiful creation of silk brocade etched with chrysanthemums, which symbolized longevity, and gold dragons, which stood for strength.

Looking at it was like immersing herself in a pool of memory: she and Travis using the elements of the ceremony that had spoken to them most profoundly, twining them with Western traditions, then making the end product their own. They had especially embraced the part about serving tea to each other's families since the gesture denoted acceptance and appreciation, although it had only been afterward that Mei had discovered his mom and dad had not come to terms with their union and had only been going through those motions.

Just as hers had.

When she touched the dress, the material felt like thick, luxurious nectar against her fingers, and the happiness and excitement, the optimism of that day, spilled over her once again.

Her mom's voice came from behind her. "He wants you to wear it this evening."

A million questions competed to be first out of her mouth, but none of them materialized.

Her mother stepped forward, holding hands with Mei. "Your father and I are doing this for you. When Travis arranged everything, he seemed...different."

So I haven't been imagining everything, Mei said to herself. *Travis's turnaround hasn't just been a product of wishful thinking. It's real.*

Her head spun, but she held herself together, taking a long-overdue stand. "You're ready to finally accept him?"

"Oh, Mei." Her mom's smile was wistful. "Your father

and I have always wanted you to live a full, rich life—that's why we left Hong Kong before China took it over, because we knew you would shine here, in a place where you could be free to succeed. Many people back home were so concerned about their quality of life after the transition. We all wondered things, like how many children each family would be able to have. We worried about our freedoms."

Her mom paused, gaze distant. "So we acted early since we knew we would have to wait a long time to obtain visas. Seven-and-a-half years, it turned out. But every moment was worth securing you more choices here than you children would have had back there."

"But you didn't like all the choices I made."

"It's true we weren't always convinced that Travis was the best for you, but…"

"But now?"

The older woman guided Mei to face the dress on the bed. It flowed over the coverlet like a bold wish.

"Now," Mom said, "he's asking for another opportunity. He approached your father and me, looking for support in this, and we ended up giving it. When it comes down to it, Mei, turning our backs on him would be like doing the same to you and Isabel."

And the new baby you're going to love, Mei added.

"I never wanted to give up on him, either," she said, unable to take her eyes off the dress.

When she touched the silk brocade cloth, the sensation was once again akin to hearing an old song that had been playing on the radio during a first kiss, a first commitment.

"'Tell me and I'll forget,'" her mom said. "'Show me and I may remember. Involve me and I'll understand.'"

The proverb reflected what Travis had in mind: recreating the tea ceremony.

Recreating all the hope they'd possessed once upon a time?

"Reaffirming what you mean to each other," her mom added. "I only hope it works."

Holding back tears, Mei stared at the dress, knowing in her heart what she wanted to do.

She picked it up, accepting it.

Behind her, she heard her mother leaving the room, quietly shutting the door behind her.

Mei shed her baggy pants and blouse, donning the red creation. It whispered over her skin, making her feel beautiful. After clasping the looped frog buttons at her collar, she unbound her hair from its band at the nape of her neck, spread it over her shoulders and took a moment before she walked out of the room, escorted by the mad cadence of her pulse.

A bride, she thought.

A new journey.

Heading down the stairs, she knew what to expect from the ceremony in general, but was nonetheless slightly terrified of what might come afterward. Experience wouldn't let her forget.

Broken promises that had been made today?

A marriage shattered beyond repair if both of them didn't live up to their new vows?

After all, how many chances would they get?

When she entered the living room, she found it full of

familiar faces: Uncle Kenneth and Aunt Stephanie, her three brothers and their wives, even both sets of grandparents. Cousin Li was there, too, garbed in her own red dress because she was a "lucky woman"—one who was already successful in marriage.

And sitting in her oldest brother Gary's lap was Isabel, decked out in a white Western wedding-type frock, her hair decorated with a flower garland, her face boasting a wide smile.

Then someone else walked into the room from the hallway.

Travis, dressed in his best suit, which stretched over his wide shoulders and made him look like a prince who'd come to claim her.

Blinding love enveloped Mei; all she could see was him, the father of her children, both present and future. The man she was always going to love no matter what happened to them.

He came forward to take her hands, his palms roughly textured against hers.

"I'm here to take you and Isabel back to our own home," he said, declaring for her, just as a groom should do during a wedding day.

His statement warmed her to the point where she was shaped into a woman formed just for him. Even all the doubts that riddled her were submerged and encased for the time being.

She was his and always would be.

And she kept repeating that, leaving no room for unwelcome thoughts. Not tonight, with him gazing at her with such overwhelming love....

Li came forward, breaking the moment apart. "Now, wait. There's some bargaining to be done."

Her cousin was obviously taking the place of the bridesmaids, who, in Travis and Mei's original version of the ritual, had created tasks for the groom to complete before he could ultimately pay for his wife and carry her away. In the spirit of their first tea ceremony, this one clearly wouldn't follow strict traditions, but it would pay homage to them.

Respectful rule breaking, Mei thought. It was so Travis.

They went through the charade of Li asking him to do things like counting each grain of rice in a pile on a tray, then answering a string of trivia questions about Mei.

All the while, he never took his gaze off his bride, and a quiver rocked her.

He hadn't needed to go through all of this—laying his soul bare in front of her family and basically admitting that he needed to start over with Mei and Isabel. He'd gone the extra mile.

And she was won over.

Bowled over.

Now Travis and she kneeled in front of her seated parents—Mei in front of her father and Travis in front of her mother—presenting the cups of tea with both hands, addressing their elders by their proper names in a show of gratitude.

For a moment, Mei's stomach knotted; in spite of the talk with her mother earlier, she had an awful vision of Mom or Dad refusing to drink, which would've meant they were opposed to the union.

But they hadn't caused a humiliating loss of face back

at the wedding, and they didn't do it now. Thank God they realized how much Mei loved Travis, and they accepted the cups with both hands and drank.

Travis's arm brushed against hers, and she knew what he had to be thinking. *Another step, Mei.*

Another step. Did it matter that Mei had already noticed that her mother had included lotus seeds and red dates in the brew? The ingredients made Mei anxious, because they signified the hope that their marriage would be fruitful.

Steeped with emotion, she wanted to blurt out the news about the baby. But that was between her and Travis, a moment to be celebrated in private, because this time they would be reunited forever. This ceremony's vows would mean everything.

They *had* to.

They continued to serve tea for her family, from the oldest on down, and in return, the elders presented Mei and Travis with red envelopes.

"This is too much," she said, surprised as she held the first gift. "Lucky" envelopes usually contained money and/or jewelry for a new couple.

"I requested only a couple of symbolic dollars for presents," Travis said as everyone else laughed softly.

Obviously, they were all in on the specifics of the altered ceremony. But she didn't feel left out; instead, she liked seeing him as almost a part of the close family.

No, actually, she loved it. She could hardly even believe it was happening.

"You have all the riches you need," Li said, offering a light touch to the end of the ceremony.

Obviously sensing it was over, Isabel put down her teacup and hopped on Mei's lap; she couldn't stop staring wide-eyed at her mother's red dress. "Are we done now?"

Laugher filled the room again, and Mei kissed her daughter's forehead.

"There's usually more to go," Travis said. "Back when we got married, this was where I showed off my dowry items, including a roast pig."

"Then," Cousin Li interjected, "after we ate, the bride's family gave some of the pig back to the groom for *his* family."

"Are we eating pig now?" Isabel asked.

Travis's gaze locked onto Mei's. "No, not now, Izzy."

Mei's blood gave a lurch in her veins. Would they be alone after this?

Would she finally be able to tell him about their new child? Because it was time. Finally time.

Even so, the little voice returned, saying, *Are you sure about that?*

Anticipation jabbed at her. She kept telling herself it *was* time. Because if not now, when?

Travis put his hand on Mei's waist, then stood, bringing her with him. "Thank you for your hospitality. For everything."

Mei's father grew serious. "Take care of my daughter."

With a bowing nod that told Mei he had probably talked with her father to a great extent before the ceremony, Travis indicated that he definitely would.

Then he slipped his arm around Mei, and she could feel the vow there, too.

"Can we have ice cream?" Isabel said.

Mei's mother motioned for the girl to come to her, and when Isabel did, the older woman picked her up, settling the child on her lap.

"Izzy," said Mrs. Chang, "I'm going to keep you here tonight with us, and we can play dress-up and eat lots of ice cream."

The four-year-old clapped her hands, completely bought.

Although Mei would never turn down a moment with her daughter, she needed to be alone with her husband.

Still, she started to ask her mom if it was okay, but the other woman was already exchanging a secretive glance with Travis.

They'd arranged this. He'd thought of every detail.

But what would he think when they got back home and she told him that they were about to be parents again?

After Travis had thanked all Mei's relatives for the part they'd played in the recommitment ceremony, he swept his wife into his arms and carried her out of her parents' home and to the dusky parking lot where his pickup sat.

"Your chariot awaits," he said, placing her carefully on the weathered vinyl seat. "Not the fanciest conveyance, but it's dependable."

She sat there in her gorgeous red dress, her purse in her lap, her black hair falling over her shoulders. He itched to gather it in his hand and allow it to rain over his fingers.

"I can't believe you went through all this work," she said softly.

"I did it to show you and your family that I mean what I say. I'm back for good. A new man."

Her lips parted, as if she was about to say something

else, but when they heard a woman's voice raised in gaiety from the direction of the condo, Mei lowered her gaze.

He wished she would come right out and just say it. She could be *too* cautious of how her words might affect others. Her parents had raised her well—that was a big point of the tea ceremony itself, showing respect and appreciation to her parents and family for that—but Travis wanted to hear what she was thinking, not just guess.

"Mei?" he asked.

"Wait a sec." She glanced up, shooting her gaze at something behind him.

He turned to see Cousin Li escorting Great-Grandfather and Great-Grandmother Chang to her compact car. They all waved at each other, and Li even blew a kiss.

"All right, then," he said, turning back to Mei after acknowledging Li's gesture. "Homeward bound?"

He thrilled to the eager gleam in her eyes, then shut her door and went to his side and climbed in, his heart full.

But…also a little hollow, because he could do so much more than this.

After shrugging off his jacket—too damned confining—then starting the engine, he pulled out of the small parking lot as Li and the grandparents kept waving. Then, once on the bush-lined street leading to the heart of Placid Valley, Mei rested her head back against the seat.

"You did it again," she said. "You amazed me."

"It wasn't so much work. I invited the key players at last night's party and they dropped everything to be here. Your mom helped out a lot with the preparations."

"Travis, I'm not talking about the work you put into it." She angled her face toward him. "There aren't many men out there who would've put themselves on the line like you did. Some guys would've even considered it a blow to their pride to go in front of their wife's family to admit that they wanted to start a marriage over again."

"When I'm wrong, I'm wrong." He draped a hand on the wheel as they neared the corner, where a neighborhood drugstore stood.

"It was…" Mei abruptly covered her face with her hands and turned forward. "I'm sorry. I'm just getting so emotional."

Her pain was his, and he immediately pulled over into the drugstore's parking lot, then cut the engine.

"Darlin'…" He undid his seat belt and scooped her into his arms, and she leaned her face into his chest.

He felt tears against his white button-down. This was where he would start paying for not going all the way, right? Maybe she sensed that his recommitment only went so far.

As far as his fear would allow.

"Just look at me," she said, using a fist to dab at her cheeks. "What a mess. And I'm not talking about running mascara, either."

"I know—you're a waterproof kind of gal." The attempt at humor fell flat. "You're never a mess, Mei. You're the most unruffled, levelheaded woman in existence."

"Hardly levelheaded. At least lately. All I do is cry…."

She sniffed, and he searched the cab for a tissue. What he found, though, were a few unused fast-food napkins stuck between the seats, and he yanked those out and dried her eyes.

Earlier, in the midst of slyly making the arrangements needed for the tea ceremony, he'd also tried to memorize the poem they'd used at their actual nuptials in the church. He'd gotten the sentiments out of the *I Ching* years ago, but the lyrical lines had struck him anew today.

After she was more composed, he put a finger under her chin, then lifted her gaze to his, knowing what she needed to hear.

What *he* needed to believe, too.

"'When two people are as one,'" he said, "'in their inmost hearts, they shatter even the strength of iron or bronze.'"

The glow in his wife's eyes told him that she realized what was going on, and in that shared bubble of knowledge, it seemed as if they were the old Travis and Mei, ready to embark on a perfect life together, determined to let nothing stand in their way.

"'And when two people understand each other,'" she continued, "'in their inmost hearts, their words are sweet and strong, like the fragrance of orchids.'"

In his mind's eye, he saw her swathed in that veil she'd worn, the tulle haloed around her upswept hair, casting her in angelic grace.

Canting forward, she pressed her lips to his. Soft, like a tiny winged thing looking for a place to settle.

He was on such an emotional high that the mere feel of her caused him to deepen the kiss, his mouth covering hers, their lips parting, their tongues meeting and exploring.

Head filling with static, he lost all sense of reality, devouring her instead. He wanted a honeymoon, a true break from all the buffers that kept separating them when all they were trying to do was find each other again.

He drew his hand from her face down her neck, his fingers hitching on her high collar. Silk—it didn't even offer competition for the smoothness of her skin—

A metallic ringing sound tickled his perception, but he chalked that up to his building arousal. Yet it kept hammering at him, and when he felt Mei pull away, he came back to his senses.

Trying to breathe again, he realized it was his phone, which he'd stuck in his suit pocket earlier and then turned on again after the ceremony had concluded.

A bolt of excitement scrambled everything, maybe because he was so used to anticipating calls for help from the battalion chief….

Whatever the reason, he found himself reaching for that phone, then checking the ID screen.

And, God help him, but when he saw that it was the chief calling, even after Travis had made it clear that he wouldn't be taking calls on vacation, he started to answer that phone.

Yes, just as if he was watching out of body, he saw himself in the midst of a reconciliation with his wife and going to push the answer button in slow, inevitable motion. He even felt a sense of relief that he was being summoned again….

Mei's expression fell, devastated.

He might as well have been staring longingly at a fire on TV…or even jumping out of the truck to haul ass to a real one.

And, most unforgivably of all, he was doing it after recommitting himself to Mei.

An apology on the tip of his tongue, he gently grabbed Mei's arms because the damage in her gaze horrified him.

"It was habit," he said, knowing only now that shaking it wouldn't be easy at all.

"Habit?" She shook her head. "That doesn't explain the look in your eyes."

He couldn't deny that he'd felt the same rush, the same hunger from when he'd watched that TV fire, the same addiction that had lured him to the station when it would've been much smarter to stay away.

"I'll go to counseling," he said, but he wondered if he truly meant it or if he was just saying anything to keep her with him. "We'll find someone to talk to and I'll—"

"Was it the chief?"

He swallowed. "Yes."

"Then maybe you should just return the call and go to the station," she said, voice numb.

His world went bleak and black, as if he'd been sideswiped. But then, gradually, his wife materialized before him again.

A destroyed Mei.

"You want to do it," she said. "Please don't lie to me about that, Travis."

Her words weren't angry or accusatory. No, they were accepting, as if she'd come to the end of a road, found that it was a dead end and had a long way to travel back to a place that would shelter her.

He dropped his hands away from her arms. "But…"

She hesitated, and he could tell that she was holding back. But then she fisted her hands on her lap, against the red dress that had symbolized so much.

"I have to draw the line somewhere," she said, "no matter how tempted I am. Otherwise, this is just going to go on and on."

And, with that, she secured her purse, opened the door and climbed out of the truck into the hovering dusk, already walking back in the direction of her parents' condo, where they'd left her car.

Another ultimatum, tearing around inside his head, ripping him apart second by second.

"If you go this time," she'd said before, "don't come back."

Watching her walk away from him, Travis realized that he never truly *had* come back.

Chapter Eleven

It had only taken Mei fifteen anesthetized minutes to walk through the falling night and back to her parents' place since she and Travis hadn't driven too far.

All the same, she'd been keenly aware that he was following her in his pickup, keeping a distance.

But she couldn't turn around for a ride back to the apartment—a place she had started thinking of as a real family home again. Even if it killed her, he had to know that she wouldn't accept anything less than what all their vows had promised.

Isabel and the baby needed her to fight for that.

And…well, *she* needed it, too.

She'd spent so much of her energy asserting herself with her family that she'd allowed her relationship with Travis to go by the wayside.

But now she was standing up to whatever was pulling her and her husband apart.

Denying the urge to just turn around and go back into his vehicle, to be with the only man she would ever love, Mei came to the parking lot, where her silver car was parked. There, she unlocked the vehicle, then slid into the front seat and placed her hands on the wheel.

Wait—should she go inside her parents' condo to get Isabel and take her home?

No. Why upset her daughter when she already expected to have a happy night with her grandparents?

While starting the engine and going through the motions of putting her car in Reverse, Mei caught a glimpse of Travis's idling pickup in the side mirror.

Don't look at him, she thought. *Don't lose what strength you have right now....*

Yet she couldn't win this one, and she glanced at him one last painful time.

He was leaning over the wheel, his tie askew, his hair disheveled, as if he'd been running his hand through it.

Travis, the man who kept breaking her heart over and over again.

I love you, she thought, *but I love our kids too much for you to keep putting us in second place to something that owns you.*

With all her will, she gave the car some gas and headed toward the parking lot's entrance. Then, stopping before she drove onto the road and left Travis behind, she hesitated, maybe because she thought something might miraculously change....

But when nothing did—not the state of the world, not

even her mind—Mei left, and Travis's pickup grew smaller and smaller in her rearview mirror.

On the way home, she didn't even remember driving. In fact, she merely discovered herself standing in the middle of the empty apartment in what seemed like the passing of a minute.

Feeling just as hollow as the silent spaces, she went past the shelves in the family room that Travis hadn't finished bolting to the wall, then moved toward the hallway.

She would deal with yet another unfinished project of his in the morning.

Then, once in her bedroom, she took off the red dress because she couldn't stand the failure of it and folded the material as if it was a flag taken down at nightfall. She stored it at the back of a closet shelf where it wouldn't mock her anymore.

All the while, realization pounded away at her.

It had happened. The worst-case scenario.

Her own nightmare.

But admitting it didn't make her feel any better as she opened up one of Travis's drawers and took out a shirt. Burying her face in it, she was too shell-shocked to do anything but inhale the scent woven into the fabric.

Everything had been going so well. What had happened?

And where was he? Had he already gone back to the station, where he'd found himself the other day, even while on vacation?

Pelted by questions, by regrets, Mei pulled the shirt over her head and then lay down on the bed, her legs bent, her arms wrapped around her midsection.

There, on just one of the places where they had tried

to piece things back together, she tried to understand why everything had fallen apart.

Although Mei slept with one ear trained to hear the front door opening during the night, she didn't catch any sign of Travis returning.

Yet what would she have done if he *had* come back? Would she have possessed the inner strength to stick to her guns?

Yes, she thought, because they were at a point of no return.

All the same, when the sky was still predawn dark, she nursed a sick stomach in the bathroom, then called Travis's battalion chief to see if he'd indeed reported for duty. It wasn't that she was keeping tabs on him so much as merely wanting to know that he was somewhere safe.

In spite of the chief's suspicious tone of voice—he could probably sense yet another casualty of the job in the way Mei and Travis weren't talking to each other yet again—he told her no. Travis had called back, but he hadn't accepted the offer of volunteer hours. The chief even apologized for contacting him, citing that he'd lost the note he'd scribbled to himself to cross Travis off his list until his vacation was over.

Mei didn't chastise the boss about that. Instead, she hung up the phone, guessing that Travis had probably gone back to Jed's, since he'd been staying there during the aftermath of the first ultimatum.

Yet one fact kept skipping through her head: Travis hadn't accepted those volunteer hours.

A twang of hope plucked her heartbeat into motion

again. If he had wanted to spite her, he could have done it. Or he could have just thrown in the towel and figured he'd lost his bid to win Mei over, anyway, so he would just go back to someplace that wanted him—the firehouse.

But…he hadn't.

He had stayed away, even though the itch to report for duty must've been overwhelming.

Slightly soothed by the notion—even if was just speculation on her part—Mei crawled back into bed and tried to get some sleep.

And she did get it, waking hours later—maybe her body and the baby needed it?—and reaching for the phone to call her mother. Mei wanted to check on Isabel while avoiding any lighthearted questions from her unknowing mom about how Travis was doing during this tea-ceremony honeymoon phase.

Mei couldn't talk about it yet—not without breaking down.

After greeting her mother, thanking her again for all her work yesterday and then asking to talk to Isabel, her daughter came on the phone. They chatted about how Grandma was going to take her to school today and stay to volunteer in the classroom.

Mei barely held it together. How was she going to tell Isabel about this?

After making sure the little girl knew just how much both of her parents loved her, Mei hung up, ill. She even went to the bathroom again because she was so dizzy and nauseous.

Following a slight bout with her upset stomach, she looked at herself in the mirror, spying a pale, wan imitation of the woman she had tried so hard to be.

But was she *really* seeing the person she was now? Seriously?

Mei got ready for the day, erasing all traces of that victim in the mirror, resolving to go on with life right away. It hurt like the gravest of pains, but she forced herself to check the Baby Boom-Boom Web site and set to work on a few new orders, creating more stock by fashioning bibs with little ducklings decorating them.

Yet concentrating on her job ultimately proved impossible.

Just before noon, she wandered out of the apartment and to the street, where she headed to the one place where she knew she would find some peace.

The Suds Club was in pre-*Flamingo Beach* chaos, with everyone taking care of her wash before the soap started. The normalcy of the activity felt good to Mei, allowing her a fair chance to forget Travis.

As if she could.

But with Liam McCree working away at his computer in the corner and Evina and Vivian getting the last of their conversation in before the first scene began, Mei at least felt as if she weren't alone anymore.

They welcomed her, and Mei took her place among her pals, keeping an eye out for Jenny, who hadn't arrived yet.

Fifteen minutes passed, and still no Jenny. Mei realized just how much she wanted to talk with her friend in particular.

When Jenny finally showed up and claimed the seat next to Mei's during a commercial break, her friend wasn't herself.

"Hey," she said, her voice oddly monotone. Very not-Jenny.

Mei glanced at her, noticing that she looked very not-Jenny, as well. There were faint pink circles under her eyes, and she wasn't dressed like the usual fashion plate. Instead, she wore boring pants and an untucked polka-dot blouse, as if she'd gotten dressed in too much of a hurry to care about the details.

"How're you doing?" Mei asked, her own problems forgotten in the face of what she was seeing here. It looked as if her friend had been crying—an activity hormonal Mei knew all too well lately.

Jenny pointed to herself. Who me? Then presented a smile that was so clearly forced that Mei frowned.

Reacting to Mei's response, the other woman shrugged, muttering, "Ridiculous workload today. But that's what I get for going out of town."

Then she nodded toward the TV, and Mei knew a diversion when she saw one. Jenny didn't want to talk about whatever was bugging her.

While they continued watching, Mei couldn't stop sneaking loaded looks over at Jenny. And when the hour ended and everyone got up to finish their wash and go home, Mei and Jenny walked out the door together, the other woman barely giving McCree a glance in his corner.

Yes, it was definitely a strange day.

They passed a small Italian restaurant named Amati's, its sidewalk tables crowded with lunch customers under the warm sun. The scent of garlic wafted out, unsettling Mei's stomach yet again.

She rubbed it, as if to calm her child…and herself. "Is everything all right, Jen?"

"Sure, yeah, but I was going to ask you the same thing."

Their steps slowed just after the restaurant, and Mei put on a brave face. But the minute she opened her mouth to talk, she had to stop herself as dammed-up sorrow rushed her.

"Oh, honey," Jenny said, patting Mei's back. "Travis?"

She nodded, waiting until she had herself under control before she even attempted another sentence.

Meanwhile, Jenny seethed. "Let me guess—he went back to work and you haven't seen him for days now."

Finally, Mei could talk, but her voice wobbled. "He got a volunteer call—"

"I knew it."

"No, it's not that." That rogue spark of hope lit through her, even though it didn't exactly catch and burn brighter. "Travis didn't accept the call this time."

"That's great!" Jenny knitted her brows. "Then why so blue?"

"It's…" What? How could she fully explain that yearning she always saw in Travis's eyes—a demon not even she could drive out?

But she tried, anyway, then attempted to illustrate everything else: The progress she'd thought they'd made. The definite anticipation of a new child added to the mix. The tea ceremony. The summons for him to return to the fray, which had driven home just how far they *hadn't* come.

By the time Mei was done, Jenny had her head down, watching the sidewalk.

It didn't take long for Mei to realize her friend was trying not to cry.

"Jenny?"

The other woman held up a hand and shook her head. Then, after a few more seconds, she said, "It'll pass. Don't worry."

Mei waited, her hand on her friend's arm. She'd never seen her like this. Ever. Not lively, put-everything-into-perspective Jenny.

Finally, the other woman steadied herself, looking up, even though she wouldn't make eye contact with Mei.

"You're the only person I'm going to tell, because, really, I don't want to make a big deal out of this when it might not be anything at all."

Apprehension gripped Mei. "What is it?"

Jenny vaguely motioned toward her chest, wetness springing to her eyes. "A lump. The doctor found one this morning during my annual appointment."

"No." Mei's stomach tightened again. Not Jenny. No. "Is there anything I can do?"

Jenny laughed, but it wasn't convincing. "Tell me that it'll turn out to be nothing."

"Maybe it will."

Jenny met Mei's gaze, then overdid a smile. Now *she* was trying to be brave. "That's why I'm not going to tell my parents or anyone else, all right? I'm just going to have my mammogram as soon as they can get me one and then I'll wait for the results."

Her courageous attempt fisted Mei's heart. "You just tell me what you need, and I'll come running. Don't ever hesitate to ask."

"Sure, that's really kind of you, Mei. But nothing's going to come of it." She blew out a breath and resumed walking, just as if she were leaving her confession behind. "I guess this is what happens when you forget to give yourself frequent self-exams, huh? Genius."

Mei kept her hand on Jenny's arm, watching the other woman for any signs of breakage.

And, after she walked her friend back to her apartment and made sure she was truly okay, Mei thought about how fragile life really was, and how one doctor's appointment could turn it all around.

Then she thought of Travis, who was out there somewhere while their own lives flew by all too quickly.

On the other side of town, Travis walked through the door of a modest little granny cottage in the back of a bigger shingle house, then sat on a tweed couch that had seen better days.

Jed, who'd rented this place from an elderly couple for years—ever since his divorce—looked away from the TV.

As the sounds from some ultimate fighting challenge blared, the men didn't say anything to each other. Not until Travis pulled out his phone to check the message screen for about the fiftieth time since arriving here last night.

"Don't tell me," his friend said. "Mei hasn't called."

Travis shook his head and put the phone on the cushion next to him. "No big shock, I suppose. She put her foot down for probably the last time yesterday. I tested her ultimatum by coming back to her the first time, she gave me a second chance, and I blew it. End of story."

Jed turned back to the screen, tapped his fingers on the

armrest of his lived-in recliner, then used the remote to mute the TV.

"Dammit, Trav. You're killin' me."

At his friend's sympathy, Travis's heart dropped into his stomach, where all the acids eroded it. Yeah, this was the same Travis who'd ranked second in the fire academy. The same man who met every emergency head-on...

He couldn't handle something that many other people found so simple.

Love.

Jed leaned forward. "Man, you've looked at that dumb phone once every thirty seconds, and I wasn't even with you on whatever errand you just ran, or out here to watch you on the couch last night. I'll bet you slept with the thing in your hand, didn't you?"

"You're not too far off the mark. I kept the phone within easy reach on the floor."

Jed cursed under his breath, then said, "Do you think you can make it ring just with your magic eyes?"

Travis ignored Jed's forthrightness: his buddy had slept in on his day off, and he always woke up rusty, even when a station alarm summoned them to action. But maybe, this time, there was an even better reason.

"If you're sore about that hot-and-heavy date I interrupted when I called yesterday," Travis said, "I'm sorry."

"You'd better be. I've been aching from sexual frustration all damned day."

"I told you I could stay somewhere else."

"But pal that I am, I insisted you come over, and as a result, I ended up getting a good-night smooch by my lady friend's car instead of something more in the bedroom."

Travis slumped on the couch. "Great. How much of a sad sack am I to make my friend lose out on a sure thing?"

"Pretty pitiful." Jed got up from his recliner and waded through some free weights strewn across the floor on the way to the kitchen. "Jeez, just look at you."

No way. Travis hadn't dared to even peer in a mirror lately, but he suspected the decimation. He *felt* it.

Jed continued. "You can't give a woman that kind of power. Take the divorce over the loss of your dignity. *I* did."

The casual advice made him bristle. "If you could go back and try to fix your marriage, what would you do?"

His friend opened a pantry cupboard, then thought for a moment. Then he held up a finger. "I'd make sure we had a prenuptial agreement that didn't kick my ass in the end."

"That's helpful."

"Hey, what can I say? Maybe our type isn't meant to be married. It takes a strong woman to deal with our jobs, and Mei obviously can't do it."

Anger roared through Travis at the slight to his wife. Or maybe it was rage at himself.

"When we got married, she didn't sign on for this job," he said. "She didn't realize that I'd be this way, but she supported me until she couldn't anymore."

"Then why the hell do you still do it?"

Travis flinched. Yeah. Why?

But he knew, and every reason slapped at him, merging with what he'd discussed with the psychologist this morning during the errand Jed had referred to.

"Why?" Travis repeated. "There're a lot of reasons. First of all, my mom died in a fire."

Jed sank back against the counter, giving a low whistle. "I didn't know."

Travis nodded at the unspoken condolences. "But there's more to it." He rested his head on the couch, staring at the ceiling. "Bottom line? I really do like being there in every way for others, especially for my wife and child. I like to protect them. This job… It's not like any other. At the end of the day, you know you've made things a lot better. You know you've done some real good out there."

As Travis glanced at Jed, a wry smile lit over his friend's mouth, but he didn't say anything. Still, Travis knew his friend understood completely.

"Mei…" he continued, throat tightened by a stinging heat. He chased it away with a pause. "I like how she looks at me when I get home from a shift—as if every time is a miracle because I came back. Would she get that same thankful relief in her eyes if I was just coming home from an office?"

"No," Jed said softly.

Travis exhaled, then said, "She's proud of what I can do. How would it feel to lose that?"

A distant look claimed his friend's gaze. "Back in the Stone Age, when I was married, I used to love how Amy curled up to me when I crawled into bed. Even when she was sleeping, she would wrap her arms around me. Then she'd wake up, and that was all shot to hell."

"I guess we all need to wake up at some point."

Silence draped the atmosphere until Jed stood away from the counter.

"I get it. That's why you've been staring at your

phone—because things haven't gone to Hades in a hand-basket for you yet. At least not entirely."

His comrade glanced at his own phone as it sat on the counter, mute, his yearning almost palpable.

That's when Travis decided to be entirely honest, to fully commit as he hadn't before, because he wasn't going to be like Jed.

"I went to a psychologist this morning," he said.

Jed's eyes widened.

Travis raised a finger. "May the powers that be help you if word of this gets out."

"No, I…"

His friend looked more curious than anything, and that was a huge relief.

"What was it like?" Jed asked.

"Way less painful than I ever thought. I found Dr. Anders on the Internet. She's been working with the department, and she told me to stop by first thing today, since she had a cancellation. It was funny, though—I always thought head doctors were a waste of time until I was sitting across from her. Then I was talking, and it wasn't awful."

"Really? It wasn't that bad?"

"Not at all."

In fact, it was nothing compared to the possibility of losing Mei and Isabel.

"What was it…like?" Jed asked.

"Well, we discussed the reasons I contacted her. Then she admitted that she'd arranged to see me before she usually comes in for the day. She said not many firefighters take the county up on getting the support they need, but whenever one contacts her, she goes out of her way for them."

"It wasn't all touchy-feely?"

"Nah. I asked a lot of questions and told her to be straight with me about what she saw us working on in the future. And she was honest. But she was adamant about my coming back for more."

"You made another appointment?"

"Yeah. I mean, in the back of my mind, I'd kind of hoped one visit would do it. And I was thinking it might impress Mei, too, but then I caught myself."

Travis folded his arms over his chest, then loosened up at the defensive gesture.

He'd made the mistake of thinking that time was the only sacrifice he needed to make for his family, but he realized that a token visit to therapy was a repeat of that error.

Jed started to say something else, then frowned, going into the kitchen and digging through the cupboard.

Travis wondered if his coworker had been about to ask for Dr. Anders's number or something—maybe just to talk about the divorce—but he didn't pursue it.

If Jed wanted to come around, he would.

His friend grabbed a protein bar and headed toward the back, where his bedroom waited. He was probably intending to take a nap since he'd stayed up half the night trying to cheer Travis up with lame jokes.

"So you feel better?" Jed asked as he neared the hallway.

"I feel…" What? More prepared to be the man Mei and Isabel really needed at home?

Instead, Travis merely said, "I feel better."

Thoughtful, Jed retreated, his bedroom door shutting behind him, leaving Travis alone.

He inspected his surroundings—a bachelor pad in its

finest form. A laptop computer hooked up willy-nilly on the kitchen counter. A grounds-choked coffeemaker in the kitchen. A pristine stereo system. A remote control always kept within easy reach of the recliner.

Alone, he thought. Without the woman and child he loved more than anything.

Utter horror swamped Travis. So did the craving to go back home, no matter what the consequences. Because when he thought of how it smelled there—of clean sheets and Mei's skin—he missed it deeply. And when he imagined Isabel's stuffed animals covering her in bed at night and when he pictured holding Mei against him as they sat on their clean couch in peaceful silence...

He leaned forward, elbows on knees, face in hands.

Dammit. Dammit all.

Shoving his hands through his hair, he sat back up and jammed the remote at the television to turn it off. Then he flopped onto his back, thinking he should catch a nap also and wake up with some better ideas about how to approach things.

Besides, he went back on shift tomorrow, and he needed all the rest he could get.

But even as that notion trailed off, he realized that the firehouse wasn't the place he wanted to be most of all, and maybe that's why he hadn't entertained any second thoughts about accepting that volunteer call last night....

Mercifully, sleep came quickly, as if to shut everything else out. However, the nightmares came, too, just as if he'd left open a door for them to enter.

Fires...

Beams slamming down from the roof, crashing, crushing...

That hand reaching, Travis reaching back and—

This time, as if riding the glass surface of the dream, Travis reared back his fist and plunged through it, shattering everything.

He grabbed on to that hand, gripping it, pulling with all his might to bring her out of the charred rubble and into safety.

But then...

What he found made him spring up, stinging with sweat, his chest banded together and making it hard to suck in oxygen. He was even still reaching out, but this time it was for a hand that wasn't there.

A touch that had brought him out of the nightmares before.

Mei.

Wiping at his eyes, he allowed the final, adrenaline-fused image to settle into his brain, embedding itself there.

Lying back down, he waited until his heart calmed, until his brain smoothed out enough to settle into rational thought.

Then, knowing what he had to do, Travis got off the couch, heading for the door.

He didn't have a plan, and fear was all but blinding him, but he was going back home to let Mei in through his *own* doors—the ones he'd shut in her face for the past few years.

And he could only hope she wouldn't recoil at what she found behind them.

Chapter Twelve

When Travis arrived at the apartment, Mei's car wasn't waiting in its reserved spot.

Even so, he parked outside the complex on a side street, then rushed inside the apartment itself, just in case she *was* there.

But…no.

Empty as he felt whenever his wife and daughter weren't around.

He closed the door behind him, the wood echoing with a dull thud. Near the kitchen, the smell of food from the most recent meal still haunted the air, faint yet powerful. He could imagine his daughter and wife sitting together at the table before him.

He went to it, resting a hand on the top of his usual

seat, wondering if they had looked at it during the meal and missed him.

He gazed around, absorbing the sights, pained by them: the kitchen where he could've cooked a lot for them, the floor where they'd all built those robots, the abandoned shelf project with its metal supports and wood beams looking like the skeletal remains of all his best intentions.

He tended to leave things that way, didn't he? Unfinished. Deserted because there was something more urgent that commanded his attention.

But he was here to change that.

Even if his stomach was roiling.

What's she going to do when she sees the real man she married? he kept thinking. *How's she going to react when she discovers I've been burying a coward beneath all the apparent bravery?*

He drifted to the counter, then sat on a stool. For better or worse, when Mei and Isabel returned, he was going to find out what they thought.

Exhaling in an attempt to settle his anxiety, he focused on the counter, where a shoe box waited, its lid halfway off.

Recognition warmed his heart. The memento box Mei usually kept stored in the hall closet. Had she been going through it in his absence?

Did he dare hope for that?

As he nudged the lid all the way off, he found newspaper articles blanketing the surface: clippings that mentioned his commendations and emergency situations he'd been involved with. The ink was smudged, as if the cutouts had been well handled.

He picked up a clipping, started to read it, even though

he was picturing Mei sitting here and looking at it more than absorbing the actual text.

But he hadn't even made it midway through when the lock on the front door tumbled.

Every cell in his body stretched inside out, warping into a heated frenzy, because he knew who it was.

Mei entered, her hands full of shopping bags from the fabric emporium. Her hair was haphazardly slumped in a ponytail that left more than a few strands in her face.

She was alone, and he didn't just mean that she was without Isabel. She seemed alienated altogether.

He knew the feeling, mostly because he'd caused it.

"Hi, Mei," he said softly, so as not to scare her.

Flinching, she dropped one of her bags, then her face lit up as if she'd discovered him here at home on a normal day and she was overjoyed to see him.

He smiled, too, hoping, hoping…

But a painful second afterward, as if she were remembering everything else, her expression fell to banked sorrow.

He couldn't say anything—too overcome, too stricken by being across a room from his own wife and knowing that he couldn't freely go to her.

Yet that's why he'd come here, right? So he could remedy that once and for all.

Even so, the fear… It infused his veins with its ice-cold last stand.

When he shared everything with her, would she turn away?

Would she regret marrying him even more?

He set the clipping on the counter, getting ready to give himself over entirely.

But she spoke first.

"You're staying at Jed's?"

"Yeah."

"That's good to hear." She put her bags on the floor, but she hadn't shut the door yet. "I mean, that's where I thought you might've gone, seeing as he put you up before."

"I still had some stuff there. Clothes. A shaving kit. Just in case…"

Mei nodded. "Just in case I turned you away the first time you came back."

The unspoken follow-up question just hung there: would she tell him that there was no use in trying yet again?

That there was no hope for them?

Travis wouldn't accept that. Hell no. Not when there was a shiver of longing building in the very core of him—a yearning that went so much deeper than the physical.

He couldn't live without her, and he wouldn't even try.

She still hadn't shut the door behind her, and to Travis, the gape of it loomed, symbolizing a final separation that he wouldn't accept.

He itched to shut it, just to show her—no, to show everything that had kept them apart—that he wasn't going tolerate any more partings.

"The house was so empty last night with Isabel at my parents'," she said.

Travis's pulse suspended its rhythm. Did that mean she'd wished he was here?

Was that what she was saying?

"What did you tell Isabel about us?" he asked, voice scratchy.

"Nothing. Maybe that's why I've hesitated to bring her

back here, because everything will become too real and I'll have to give her some reason."

At her confession—she hadn't given up on him after all, even though she had every reason to—he gripped the counter. For the balance he needed.

For the strength to do what he had to do.

His movement caught her gaze, and her attention fixed on the box near his hand.

She bit her lip, her palm resting on her belly, a protective gesture, and it was as if he'd broken into *her* by looking at the contents.

"I was just riffling through—" he began.

"It's okay."

Mei turned around, shut the door, and his heart nearly exploded.

Then she walked to him, closer.

Closer.

"I came upon it earlier." She stopped, then offered a wilted laugh. "I won't lie. I took it out of the closet and was going through it, seeing if there was something that would explain all this. If there was a key that would unlock all the answers."

When she closed the last few steps between them, he breathed her in.

Mei.

So near that he could run his fingers over the curve of her arm if he dared.

So warm that he had to restrain himself from leaning down to rest his mouth against her cheek.

Hands unsteady, she reached into the box, then removed the articles from the top, revealing a collection of objects beneath.

Among them, a commendation medal shined. Picking it up, she ran a reverent finger over it, and Travis felt as if she were touching him, admiring, appreciating.

His body responded, a brutal jerk to his heartbeat.

"The Commendable Merit Medal," she said, "for gallantry and bravery. You got this when you rushed into that burning apartment complex over on Basil Avenue and came out with that little girl."

Travis's gut twisted. "All I saw was Isabel in that apartment, in trouble. That's the hardest part—when the danger involves kids."

When Mei glanced at him, her eyes were moist.

Always a hero, her gaze said.

She gently set down the medal, then extracted a ragged swath of flowered material from the box.

Travis recognized it immediately, his heartbeat snagging on a memory.

"Our first date," he said. "We were walking out of the apartment you were sharing with your roommates and your dress got caught in the door."

"I was distracted. Nervous."

"You went back inside to change outfits."

"How could I go out with a torn skirt?"

Travis reached out to take the opposite edge of the swath, and they both held it, connected.

"While you were gone, I found this on the floor, and I pocketed it." He smiled. "At the end of the night, I tucked it away in one of my kitchen drawers because I already knew I wanted to keep you, whether it was just a part of your dress or more."

Almost imperceptibly, she pulled the swath closer to her, bringing his hand that much nearer to her body as her gaze locked onto his. His pulse banged at him as if hammering out a code.

Let.

Her.

In.

Now she was all but whispering, strangled. "Later, after you proposed, you showed me that you'd held on to this, and I couldn't believe it."

"I've always kept you, Mei, whether it's been inside my heart or in a memory box."

A moment pulled at them, and that inner voice cut in. *Let her all the way in or lose her....*

As they both clung to the swath, it grew taut between them, his fingers inching nearer to her...nearer...

Then the low, thready screech of ripping fabric made them both let up, and she released it, giving the swath over to him, her expression crushed.

But then he raised it, showing her only a slight tear. "Look. It held together."

At his encouraging words, she exhaled, closed her eyes, then opened them again. "It did manage, didn't it?"

Taking that as a good sign, he spread the flowered material on the counter, smoothing it out, and she ran a finger over the edge of the box.

Then she sucked in a breath.

"Remember this?" she asked, her tone reflecting more optimism now as she picked a rock out.

Just a reddened, marbled piece shaped like a star that Mei had thought was pretty. But it encapsulated just as much as the swath did.

"That day," she said, "during one of the hikes we took before…"

"Before my mom passed."

He took the memento out of her hand and weighed it in his own.

Mei watched him with such compassion that he tried to get a grip on himself.

How could she still be so open, so willingly vulnerable around the husband who could easily run into a burning building but found it impossible to share every part of himself?

"We were scrambling up that big rock," she said, "and a woman was with her friends, who were doing everything they could to encourage her to move on. But she was frozen, clutching the rock's face. Afraid of heights."

"She said it was as if something was pulling at her, making her feel as if she was going to jump."

"And you…" Mei put the rock on the counter. "You led her down to safety, reassuring her the whole way. Rescuing her before you ever even thought of being a paramedic or firefighter."

She reached out a hand, tilting her head as if almost afraid of what might happen if she actually touched him.

Her hesitation felt like a sucker punch.

But when her palm made contact with his face, her hand cupping his jaw, he realized that she truly wanted to accept everything about him.

"You've always been someone's savior, Travis," she

said. "And you always will be. I've got to come to better terms with that."

He slid off the stool, and her eyes widened—just an irrational knee-jerk reaction, as if she was afraid that maybe he was going to leave this task unfinished, too.

That maybe he was going to leave her again.

It gave him the strength to perform the bravest feat he'd ever attempted.

"I got the help I've been needing, Mei."

She blinked, then furrowed her brow. "Are you telling me that you didn't answer that overtime call? Travis, I already know that, and I—"

He tenderly gripped her arms. "I saw a therapist."

Hope flared in her eyes, flickering after the first burst like a light struggling to stay on.

"I won't go into everything right now," he added, pushing those doors of his open and allowing her a peek inside, even though the hinges of his mind screeched in resistance, "but I know what I'll need to work on. These…abandonment issues, I guess you could say."

His pulse screwed into him. Had her hero showed a weakness? What did she think of him now?

But even worse, he was beginning to fear that maybe *he* couldn't handle appearing weak in front of her….

Was that the biggest issue of all in their marriage?

Did he need Mei to see him as strong and invincible even more than he needed to be fighting back?

"Your mom left you when she died in that fire," she said. "And your father… Sometimes it might feel as if he abandoned you, too. Maybe in all your grieving, you mourned the loss of…connection?"

He closed his eyes so she couldn't see into him, but then he forced his gaze open.

Inviting her in.

Finally. Irrevocably.

"Anger took the place of any connection," he said. "Anger at the fire. That's why I think I went overboard. That's what I need to deal with."

"Travis…"

He could feel her arms stiffen under his hands, and he held his breath, all his worst nightmares about Mei gnawing at him until he felt raw.

Exposed.

"*You* need to deal with?" she asked, her tone strained, her eyes dark. "Just *you?* Travis, *I've* got a lot to learn about being married to a man who's dedicated his life to this calling. I need to change, too, and I need to be with you every step of the way."

He hadn't meant to exclude her, but he obviously had done just that.

And with the hurt he also saw anger reflected back at him—a burning scar on the mirror of his soul.

Except that mirror was in her eyes.

Dammit, this hadn't gone right at all. He should've kept hiding everything….

Maybe it was in defense, but he deflected her anguished gaze by turning the mirror back on her, hoping to God she hadn't seen too much.

"I know you've been angry, too, Mei," he said. "About being disappointed in what you thought this marriage would be. About a lot of things—including how you let down your family. But you were able to fight back with them in your own quiet, firm way. You never did that with me until recently."

"Exactly."

She sounded so wounded. God, he kept ruining things over and over again.

At the breaking point, he struggled to keep himself together, opening himself up again…just an inch.

Just a sliver.

"Can't we get the anger out of our lives once and for all?" he asked, the question tearing the air like the swath of material from her first-date dress.

He just prayed that it would hold as surely as the memento from a much brighter past.

What was Travis saying? Mei wondered. That she had some repressed anger she needed to deal with if they were really going to succeed in rebuilding?

Well, he was right—and she was willing to do just that.

Honestly, she'd learned to repress her thoughts early on with her parents, and she'd refined the technique in her American school when she'd learned to fit in by caging her true self. And, ultimately, her tendency to allow her feelings to build up while pretending nothing was bothering her had only allowed Travis's neglect of the family to go on for much longer than it should have….

Had she even been punishing him for his past behavior by keeping their baby a secret these past couple of days?

Was she *still* doing that?

At her stunned lack of response to his question, something went dark in Travis's eyes—as if she had doused the hope within him.

He slowly lowered his hands from her arms. The after-burn on her skin sent her body into chaos.

No. She wouldn't let them fail.

Not again.

"You want me to let loose on you," she said. "Just like I did with the ultimatum."

"I want you to react, Mei," he said, almost desperately. "Not leave me wondering what you think of me now."

She'd never seen him so openly emotional, and her veins tangled, tugging at her while she took in her husband's ashen gaze.

"You believe I'm going to think less of you now that you admitted to needing help?" she asked. "Is that it?"

He didn't even have to say anything. The answer was in the torment of his eyes.

Now Mei *did* get angry—at what they hadn't been able to handle. At what she was going to overcome, no matter what the odds were.

She raised a finger, emphasizing every word. "I think it takes more courage to confront our issues than you've ever had to call upon in your job. I think I was so damned afraid of losing you that I was scared to death to get angry—until it all just came out in one ugly moment—"

Her words choked off, dried in the thickness of her throat.

Jenny, she thought, recalling her friend's shattering news. The lump in her breast. All the time she might not have to live life to its fullest.

Tears pricked at Mei's eyes. Was it the hormones again?

Or maybe she'd just had enough.

"Life is too short," she said fiercely, "and we've wasted too much time already."

In the blur of her gaze, she could see him taking a step closer, as if hardly believing she accepted everything about him.

Life really was too short, she thought, brushing her fingers over her belly. And she had already robbed them of the celebration they could have been enjoying.

Her pulse thudded in her temples as she grabbed both of Travis's hands and led him out of the family room and down the hall to their room, where there was something she'd been keeping buried in a drawer.

Something she wasn't going to tuck away any longer.

She could barely even hear herself thinking, especially when she halted outside of the bathroom. Travis seemed unsure of what her intentions were.

And then he saw the bed.

His shirts were piled there because she'd gone through them this morning, just to catch the scent of him, just to grip onto a part of him that could keep her going for another day.

"It was the closet I thought I might get to you for a while," she said.

A dam of emotion broke in his eyes—a hard man crumbling right in front of her.

But she knew how to piece him together again.

Piece *them* together.

Mei went into the bathroom, then opened up her private drawer, taking out the plastic-bag-wrapped pregnancy stick. Blowing out a shuddering breath, she came back and slipped it into his hand.

He looked at it.

And looked.

Good heavens, maybe she needed to make this clearer.

Mei hugged him to her, and he glanced away from the stick, then dropped it.

Slowly, as if testing, Mei pulled him closer to her, and his hands slid to her waist, his thumbs brushing the very slight curve of her belly.

Heartbeat jumping, she looked up into his eyes.

Joy swirled there, echoing the rush of her own heartbeat.

He smiled a little, and a blast of yearning shot through her.

"Welcome home from me, Travis," she said, taking his hand and placing it on her tummy, "and welcome home from your children."

Her heart kicked its way out of her chest as she waited for him to say something.

Anything.

Chapter Thirteen

It took Travis several moments to sort through what Mei had just revealed.

Welcome home from his *children*. The pregnancy-kit stick…

When it all finally settled in his brain, he asked, "You're…?"

"Yes." Her dark liquid gaze searched his. "I'm pregnant."

Something shot upward inside of him, like a creature freed into the air.

But on its way, claws seemed to tear a path.

Could he be a better dad than he'd been to Isabel?

Mei's eyes misted over, and she loosened her grasp on his hand. "I've taken a home test. We must've conceived when I used those antibiotics for my bronchitis. I'll ask the doctor next week, but sometimes the medication can interfere with the Pill…."

"We're having a baby?" he asked, voice cracking.

She caught the emotion in his tone and bit her bottom lip, nodding.

Images of their first daughter's birth whipped into him: how Mei had squeezed his hand almost right off while he'd coached her about how to breathe. How both of them had held their ruddy, squirming little bundle of a newborn girl and honored her with his mother's middle name.

How he'd feared for the safety of their baby and subsequently fought for it so hard by going out into the world and facing its monsters….

Mei was still watching him, something akin to that same protective fear for their children shading her eyes, too.

All along, *she'd* been sheltering herself and Isabel—and this baby?—just as much as *he'd* tried to with all his extreme efforts.

I am *ready,* he thought. Ready to be there for his family, as well as the community.

"Travis?" Mei asked.

He was needlessly putting her through a tiny hell right now while he absorbed the wonderful news.

"A baby," he said, looking down at his hand on her belly and caressing it. "We're having another child."

As Mei's face bloomed with a smile that reduced him to slush, he tenderly gathered his wife in his arms again, cradling her head against his shoulder while he spoke into her soft, fragrant hair.

"Names. Have you thought of names or…?"

Mei hugged him fully, laughing slightly, the sound washing through him.

"Not yet." She paused. "I've known for a couple of days, but I wasn't sure it was the time for this kind of announcement."

"You were afraid to tell me."

"Not now. Not ever again." She nuzzled his chest. "But maybe I did do some thinking about names already."

"You've always wanted more children." He leaned his cheek against her head. This was the way it should've been for years, with them bonded together, with nothing else wrenching them apart. "You probably have pages of names written down somewhere."

"Okay, so I have a file on the computer with two lists. One for boys, one for girls."

"And…?"

As she offered each name, his heart softened with images of what their new child might be like in two years, seven…thirty, when he and Mei were older and grayer and still holding each other every night.

"I've always liked the name Abigail," Mei said. "It's got such an old-fashioned ring to it."

"Abby." Travis's smile stretched his mouth. "She'd wear ponytails and be the editor of her school newspaper."

Mei laughed again, and it sustained him.

"Or Bettina," she said. "I don't know why I like that one so much. I've always thought it was pretty."

"I'd call her Tina."

This time when his wife laughed, Travis wasn't sure if it was also a sob. But it was a good sob, because they were together again.

He knew it, she knew it.

"And boys?" he asked.

"Zachary."

She angled her face so that she was looking up at him, and he met her gaze. Her beautiful gaze—accepting of everything he'd been so wary of sharing.

He should've always known she would be there for him and not have stayed away out of fear that she might turn him away if she saw he was only human.

"I was thinking of…Charles," he said, taking that next step in his recovery, even though it seemed like the toughest one.

Mei touched Travis's face, her fingertips burning against his skin. "Your father's name."

Had he offered it because the attempt might go a long way in showing his dad that Travis wanted to mend fences?

From the way Mei was watching him, he knew that she thought so.

My soul mate, Travis thought. *Even if we can't always know exactly what each other is thinking, no one knows me better or ever will. I should've always trusted in that.*

"We could always call him Charlie," Travis said. "Or Chad or Chaz. Maybe even Chuck."

"Chuck Webb, action star."

They both laughed softly, but when Mei's fingers delicately traveled from his cheek to his jaw, the humor turned into something more.

Her lips parted, her eyes going darker with what he knew was desire.

His body responded by clutching into itself. He could never get enough of her—his Mei.

"When we made love a few nights ago," she said, her tone huskier, "I'd just taken the pregnancy test and found out about our baby. I was so happy, and I wanted you to know also. But I suppose I was still so unsure of you. So angry, too."

He recalled how she'd taken charge that night, not only with starting things but with ending them, as well. Maybe there had been a little aggression going on, yet he'd been too caught up in the bliss of sex to notice.

Mei ran her fingers down to his throat, over his jugular, which was pulsing.

"Maybe I thought keeping it secret would make me feel more in control," she said, "but it didn't feel good at all, Travis. I'd rather have been touching you like this—" she skimmed her thumb down the center of his throat "—and this."

She used her other hand to untuck the back of his shirt, then slid her fingers under the material. The second she made contact with his flesh, he jerked, the heat sizzling directly to his groin.

"Mei—" His words sawed off as she brushed her other hand down his chest.

"What?" she whispered.

"It's not too soon again?"

After all, she'd just admitted that she'd had other things in mind when they'd last had sex. Shouldn't they work their way toward their next time?

Then again, she was only being absolutely honest with him, and that was what he'd been wishing for. He would just have to trust *her* with his heart now.

And, dammit all, he would.

* * *

Was it too soon?

Unlike the last time, Mei wasn't harboring any reservations. Travis genuinely wanted another child; she'd seen it in his eyes even if his actual words had been slow in coming.

He was really back—her Travis—and there would be no separating them now.

Keeping eye contact with him, she went to the vanity table, opened the drawer, then turned her back as she extracted what she'd been keeping so secure for just the right time.

Then she came back to him, resuming her position against his body, placing her free hand on his bare back beneath his shirt. She felt the sinew, the rugged contours that she'd missed night after night.

Passion surged, shining from her center outward, exploding into pulses of hunger as she held up the diamond band.

With this ring, she thought, *I thee wed.*

Mei pressed the jewelry into his palm so he could slide it on her finger. "I'm marrying you for the last time. It started with the tea ceremony, and it'll be clinched here."

His green-gray eyes got that intense look that thrilled her, and he took her hand, poising the ring over the proper finger.

And when he slid the ring onto her finger, everything seemed to lock into place: the past clicked to its rightful position behind them, where they could look back at it in order to learn.

The future took its spot before them, where it loomed with dreams to strive for.

And the present?

It surrounded them, bringing them together in a sweet, soul-fusing embrace.

A beautiful minute passed, then Travis cupped her face as if she were something fragile to hold carefully and appreciate. She closed her eyes, anticipating the taste of his mouth on hers, her head buzzing until the sensations flowed down over her skin, bathing her with heat.

Then she felt him—his lips, touching hers so softly, taking a sip.

Pausing.

Taking another.

His deliberation drove her crazy, and she went up on her tiptoes to fully catch his mouth with hers, crushing him in urgency, wanting him with a searing need.

He moaned, and she planted her hand at the back of his head, digging her fingers into his thick hair and pulling him down to her with tender urgency.

She feasted on him, very much welcoming him back.

"Mei," he murmured against her lips before he slid his tongue into her mouth.

There, she captured his tongue with her own, engaging him, ravenous, grateful he was here again.

His face scratched against hers, leaving a flare of friction, and she pressed closer, her breasts smashed against his chest, her neck tilted back as his hand clasped what was left of her ponytail.

As they fed from each other, she slid one hand down to his waist, where she delved beneath his shirt to touch his hard abs, his ribs.

Breathless, she managed to break away from his mouth—her lips moist with his flavor.

"Let's…get rid of the shirt," she panted.

He crossed his arms, reaching down to the hem and shucking the material over his head. As the shirt slipped to the floor, Mei pushed her hands up his wide chest, under his arms. At the same time, she skimmed her mouth over one of his nipples, eager to feel it against her tongue.

He grasped her ponytail, and she reveled in his response. She hadn't gotten to do this last time. No, he had set out to please *her* by kissing her body all over, loving it, torching her from head to toe.

Circling his nipple, she brought it to a nubbed peak, sucking on it, gently teasing it between her teeth. Meanwhile, she rubbed his stomach, teasing the slight downy line that trailed from his navel to the area still covered by his jeans.

So familiar.

So wonderful to have it all back….

In his enthusiasm, he had undone her hair from its band and was running his fingers through it now.

"Enough," he said, guiding her head away from his chest and edging her toward the bed. Then he seemed to contradict himself. *"More."*

Yet she knew what he meant as the backs of her knees hit the mattress.

She kicked off her flat shoes while he made short work of her blouse, tossing it in the direction of his own discarded shirt on the floor and leaving her in only a lacy white bra.

His eyes all but glowed with the silent promises he was making for the present.

I'm going to give you some honeymoon, they said.

Shivering, she began taking off her skirt while he doffed his boots. Yet before they continued, he stopped to pay homage to her belly, running his knuckles over it.

"You can barely tell," he said.

"It'll take a bit." She thought of how it'd been more than a few months before Isabel had really started showing.

Moved by the memory, she held his hand, their fingers twining. Then he bent down to kiss her again—softer.

With all the tenderness in creation.

As their sips grew more insistent, he reached around to coax off her bra, freeing her breasts. Afterward, he guided her onto the bed, where she was cushioned by all the shirts she'd strewn over the mattress earlier.

Covered in them, Mei was surrounded by his scent, and she rode each inhalation until his essence settled inside of her. She turned her face to the side and rubbed her cheek against one piece of cloth, then used her hands to press as many as she could against her head until she was buried.

Travis laughed. "It's almost like you're playing in a bunch of flowers."

She felt that way, too, but these were much more of an aphrodisiac. "They say couples miss each other's pheromones when they're apart."

"There won't be a need for that anymore."

He crawled onto the mattress, pushing aside all the clothing except for the pieces she still hoarded.

Wanting the real thing instead, Mei let go of the shirts and turned her face so she could take in the musky scent of his nearby arm instead. Drunk on him, she kissed the skin near the crook of his elbow, a shot of desire growing to a sharp throb between her legs.

In the meantime, he worked off her lace panties with one hand: down her thighs, her calves.

All the way gone.

Then he smoothed that hand back upward, stopping at the area that ached the most, sweeping his thumb into the cleft of her.

Mei groaned as she watched him through her half-closed lids.

"It'll be much slower this time," he said, proving it by petting her with lazy strokes.

She wiggled, already wanting all of him inside of her, but she could tell he was serious about drawing out their pleasure, second by second.

And when he casually smoothed the same hand up to her breasts, she raised her arms above her head, sensuously inviting him.

Travis. Her mate. Here, forever.

Absently, she ran her thumb along the ring on her finger, overjoyed.

At the same time, Travis sketched around one breast, covering it high and low with the tips of his fingers. Mei held back another moan.

"I missed so many things about us," he said. "Things like this."

His thumb stimulated the tip, beading it to near-painful excitement. It seemed as if his hands were made for cupping her, shaping her, whipping her into madness.

She tried to contain a rising blaze but only succeeded in arching her hips as he moved on to the other breast.

When he bent down to take it into his mouth, she quivered, her skin alive.

Her whole body reborn.

After he'd worked the second breast to a peak, Travis moved down to kiss the center of Mei's stomach, then traced a hand down her belly, where their baby waited. Her skin was as silky as her white bridal dress had been.

Then he sought the damp area between her legs, and she parted for him on a soft mewl. Watching her face, he knew he was the only one who could bring her to these heights, and he would do it again and again, as long as time allowed.

He leisurely caressed her, causing her to strain against him. Her movements made her diamond ring flash in the subdued, natural light of the room, and it reminded him of how much work went into bringing the perfect, shining cut to a gem. It always started out rough, but came out gleaming in the end.

And that's how it would be with him and Mei.

He slid a finger into her, and her fevered cry aroused him even more, especially when she clutched at one of his shirts for dear life, her body rocking its way to a climax.

"I love seeing how you react," he murmured. "What kind of effect I have on your body. Your expressions."

"When…" she said, the words coming in gasps "…will I get to see you?"

If his erection had anything to say about it, the wait wouldn't be that far off.

His groin throbbed as he brought her closer and closer

to a bursting resolution. He could feel the countdown to her orgasm in him, too.

By the time she stiffened, then shuddered, Travis was painfully straining against his fly. It didn't take but a heartbeat for Mei to fix a famished gaze on him, rise up and push his clothes out of the way as she came to him.

He almost exploded right then and there.

"You've been so patient," she whispered, insinuating her hand against his arousal. "In a lot of ways."

She rubbed him through his jeans and he clenched his jaw, curbing himself. Trying and trying and trying…

But as an escalating pressure expanded to the point where he couldn't control much at all, he stood, ripping off his jeans and coming back to the bed.

Positioning both him and Mei on their sides, he lifted one of her legs over his hip, opening her for him, then prodding her.

"I love you so much," she said, looking into his eyes.

"I love you, too, Mei. I always will."

He drove into her, and they moved together, churning, the motion lifting them from where they'd been before to a new level, where they could look down and see what they had overcome.

Higher, higher…

He felt weightless now, even with her connected to him, and when she rose ahead of him, he never once thought that she would leave him behind.

Clouds…

The sky…

The thinning air where loss of gravity only lightened him even more….

Above him, he saw Mei reaching out the same hand she'd offered him so many times since he'd come back. The promise of help he hadn't taken until now—

And when he finally grasped it, she lifted him to the top, and he finally pulled her all the way inside of him, where they both flared into a clap of light, then a showering of hope.

Afterward, as they lay in each other's arms and kissed each other again, always connected, ever bonded, Travis kept a hold of her hand.

Intending never to let go.

Epilogue

Eight months later

Great-Grandfather Chang's one-hundredth birthday party was in full swing at the park in the subdivision where he lived with his wife of more than seventy-five years.

In addition to the requisite spread of noodle dishes and desserts loading down the picnic tables, there were balloons attached to the chain-link fence surrounding a baseball diamond. There were teenagers playing three-legged races that a second cousin had set up for games and activities. And there were adults visiting and sitting in lawn chairs on this warm spring weekend.

But Mei had already done her fill of meeting and greeting, and she was perfectly content on the outskirts of a group who'd gathered under an oak tree.

Children sat with their legs crossed, looking up at the man who had taken Mei's place as storyteller for a lot of previous parties.

There were even a few older Changs listening to Travis, too, these days.

He was relaying a story about how his crew had helped a man who'd reached down a bathroom sink to unclog a drain and couldn't get his hand back out.

"Firefighters aren't just called for fires, you know," he said, referring to a lot of other calls they received for Station Two, located on a very quiet side of town.

Cousin Tommy, Li's son, was naturally at Travis's side rather than engaging in a three-legged race. He was going to graduate from high school this year, and he'd announced his plans to go to Placid Valley Community College for a fire officer degree.

"What'd you have to do to get the man out?" he asked his hero eagerly.

Travis grinned at Mei, who was leaning back against the bole of a tree and lazily circling her palm over her huge belly. They would be having their son any day now.

"Well," Travis said as the children continued to worship him with their gazes. "What would *you* do?"

While Tommy thought about it, a blond six-year-old girl sitting next to Isabel in the sea of dark-headed children volunteered her own opinion.

"I'd take the sink off the wall."

Travis raised his eyebrows at his niece, who'd come with his younger sister, Julia.

As a matter of fact, all of his side of the family were here today, scattered around the grounds. Dr. Anders had aided Travis and Mei to the point where he felt comfortable enough to pursue a real relationship with his father, and gradually, they'd started to attend select gatherings.

Now Travis glanced at his dad, who was sitting in a chair next to Mei's parents on the fringes of the crowd. The older man smiled at his son, encouraging him to continue.

Travis smiled back, and Mei's heart grew to twice its normal size. He had come such a long way.

They both had.

He answered his niece. "Well, we *did* take that sink off the wall. It was the easiest way, and we got our save for the day."

As the kids started asking questions about what was in the drain and what the man's hand looked like afterward, Mei felt the baby kick.

Waving at Travis, she made the Charlie-is-getting-active face.

He translated it and quickly wrapped up the story, much to the children's disappointment. But he promised more later, and that seemed to appease them for the time being.

As they scattered, he came over to Mei, resting a hand on her ball of a stomach. Isabel scampered over, too, smiling and feeling Charlie flail around.

"Whoa," Travis said after a particularly energetic kick. "I said it once and I'll say it again—there's a soccer player in there."

She met her husband's gaze, getting lost in it—but not lost in a way that left her without options or answers.

"Love you," she mouthed to him, grinning.

He mouthed it back, and after a few seconds, he nodded toward their parents, clearly asking if she minded going over to them and allowing them to get further acquainted with Charlie, too.

"You bet," she said.

And they all went to Grandpa Charles and Grandpa and Grandma Chang, whose faces lit up at their approach.

A second-chance family, Mei thought as they gathered together in a circle, so thankful they'd all gotten to this point of forgiveness.

A loving clan who would always be there for one another.

* * * * *

Don't miss Jenny's story, the third book in
Crystal Green's new mini-series
THE SUDS CLUB
on sale September 2009 from wherever
Mills & Boon® books are sold.

Hannah's Baby
by
Cathy Gillen Thacker

Hannah Callahan stood on the porch of her childhood home, savoring the cool breeze of a perfect summer morning, watching dawn streak across the vast mountains. She had grown up in Summit, Texas, and although she had spent most of her post-college years living out of a suitcase in hotels all over the world, she was glad to leave those nomad days behind her. Glad to be starting a new chapter of her life.

A dark-green Land Rover made its way up the quiet residential street.

Hannah acknowledged the driver and wrestled her suitcase down the broad wooden steps of the prairie-style home.

Thirty-five-year-old Joe Daugherty left the motor running and met her halfway up the sidewalk. He was dressed in loose fitting trousers and a vibrant striped shirt that brought out the evergreen hue of his eyes. As always, the sheer size of his rugged six-foot-three frame dwarfed her considerably smaller body.

Hannah shifted her gaze from his broad shoulders, trying not to notice how petite she felt in his presence. She and Joe had met five months earlier. He'd come into the store, and the two of them had hit it off immediately. She'd been instantly and undeniably attracted to the sexy adventurer. He had seemed similarly interested. Had she not been so ready to settle down, and had he planned to stay in the area for more than the six months it took to research and write his book, maybe they would have gotten together. But Hannah was not interested in beginning an affair that would only have to end, so they'd relegated each other to the category of casual friend, nothing more. The fact he was going on this trip with her was a fluke, the kind of favor not likely to be repeated. She needed to remember that.

The emotion simmering inside her this morning had nothing to do with the arresting features of his masculine face, or the way the short strands of his hair gleamed against the suntanned hue of his skin. Nor did it have anything to do with the amount of time she was going to be spending with Joe Daugherty over the next week. Her racing pulse was caused by the continuing tension between her and the only family she had left. Anticipation of the events to come…

Oblivious to her tumultuous thoughts, Joe slipped his strong hand beneath hers to grip the handle on her wheeled twenty-six-inch suitcase. "This all the luggage you've got?"

Hannah nodded around the sudden lump in her throat and clasped the red canvas carryall of important papers and travel necessities closer to her body. "I just need to stop by the Mercantile and say goodbye to my dad." Try one last time to talk some sense into him.

Joe fit her suitcase next to his and shut the tailgate. "No problem." He slid behind the wheel while she jumped in to ride shotgun. He looked over his shoulder as he backed out of the drive. "We've got plenty of time."

But not enough to change her dad's mind. Hannah swallowed, beset by nerves once again. "Thanks for going with me."

Joe shrugged and flashed her a sexy half smile. "Hey. It's

not every day somebody offers me an all expense paid trip to Taiwan."

"Seriously—"

"Seriously." He sent her a brief telling look that spoke volumes about his inherently understanding nature. "You need somebody to accompany you who has a current passport and no fear of the complexities of international travel. Someone who knows that particular region of Asia, not to mention the language, and is footloose and fancy-free enough to be able to drop everything and go once you got the word it was time."

Stipulations that had narrowed the field of possible travel companions considerably. Glad he was not reading anything else into the invitation she had issued him, Hannah relaxed and settled back in her seat. "Ah, the virtues of being an adventure-loving travel writer," she teased.

Joe braked for an armadillo taking his time about crossing the road. As he waited, he grinned at her. "Versus the virtues of being a marketing whiz turned entrepreneur?"

His praise made her flush. Pretending her self-consciousness had nothing to do with him, Hannah wrinkled her nose. "You can't really call me an entrepreneur since the business I'm going to run—*if* I can ever get my dad to retire—has been in the family since Summit was founded in 1847." Since then the mountain town had gone from an isolated but beautiful trading post for ranchers and settlers to a popular getaway and tourist attraction.

The armadillo finally hit the berm. Hands clasping the wheel, Joe drove on. "The changes you want to make are good ones."

He was one of the few people who had seen Hannah's plans to turn around the slowly diminishing family business. Hannah caught a whiff of cinnamon roll as they passed the bakery. "Tell that to my dad."

"I have, a time or two." Joe pressed his lips together ruefully. "Not that he's inclined to listen to an East Coast city slicker like me."

Hannah fidgeted when they stopped at a red light. She was so ready to get to Taipei and begin her new life it was ridiculous. "You grew up in Texas."

"For the first ten years of my life—" Joe waved at a prominent rancher in a pickup truck "—but I went to school in Connecticut."

While she respected Joe's Ivy League credentials, it was the inherently respectful, compassionate way he treated everyone who crossed his path that she admired. Had he intended to stay in the beautiful Trans-Pecos area of West Texas, she might have considered seeing if the two of them could be more than friends.

Unfortunately, she knew it would never happen. He was as much a vagabond at heart as she had once been. For reasons, she suspected, that were just as elusive and privately devastating as her own.

Her mother's death and her father's recent heart attack had made her face the fact that time to address old hurts—or at the very least come to terms with them—was running out. If she wanted to heal the rift between her and her dad, the way her mother had always wanted, it had to be done soon. Whether her dad cooperated or not!

Aware the silence between them had stretched on for too long, Hannah shifted her attention back to Joe and asked casually, "When will you be done with your book?" Last spring, he'd rented a cabin just outside town and used it as a home base for his research on southwest Texas.

"It's essentially done now. I just want to take one more trip to Big Bend, to check out a couple of the hotels I missed on my earlier visits, write the magazine articles I'm going to use to promote the book, and then I'm off to Australia to start my next project."

"So you'll be leaving…?"

"Texas? Right after Labor Day."

Which meant, Hannah thought sadly, she'd rarely if ever see Joe again.

In another three weeks, he'd no longer be stopping by the Mercantile to chat up the tourists shopping there about their favorite haunts in this part of Texas. He'd no longer be teasing her, or making polite conversation with her father. Or stopping by to see if she wanted to grab some lunch at one of the cafés in town, along with whomever else their age he could round up.

Joe turned onto Main Street. The county courthouse and police station sat across from the parklike grounds of the town square, taking one whole block. Farther down, brick buildings some two hundred years old sported colorful awnings over picture windows. In the past few years, restaurants that catered to tourists and natives alike had sprung up here and there, adding to the length of the wide boulevard in the center of town. But it was the imposing Callahan Mercantile & Feed that gave Summit the Old West ambience tourists loved to photograph.

Built shortly after Texas achieved statehood, the sprawling general store still bore the original log-cabin exterior. Improvements had been made over the years, but the wooden rocking chairs scattered across the covered porch that fronted the building still beckoned a person to linger, even after purchases were made.

Joe eased his SUV into a parking space in front of the store. "Any chance the day's pastries have arrived yet?"

Hannah nodded. "My dad stops by the bakery personally every morning to pick them up before he comes in. Help yourself to whatever is there. I'll go find Dad."

Gus was in back, as she figured he would be.

At seventy, he was still a handsome man with expressive brown eyes the same shade as hers. In the two years since her mother's death, his thick straight hair had turned completely white. Gus Callahan had never been an easy man. He was set in his ways. Opinionated. He had a strong sense of right and wrong and had never been known to yield to anyone. Including Hannah.

A lump formed in her throat. Wondering when she would ever stop longing for his approval, she managed to choke out, "Dad?"

He looked up from the account statements he was sorting through.

"I'm leaving," she said wishing, once again, for a miracle.

Gus scowled and set down the stack of billing notices. He looked her square in the eye and said flatly, "It's still not too late to change your mind."

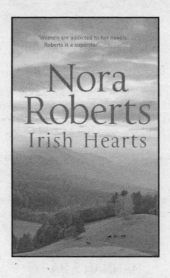

2 Books
and a surprise gift!

We would like to take this opportunity to thank you for reading this Mills & Boon® book by offering you the chance to take TWO more specially selected titles from the Special Edition series absolutely FREE! We're also making this offer to introduce you to the benefits of the Mills & Boon® Book Club™—

- ★ FREE home delivery
- ★ FREE gifts and competitions
- ★ FREE monthly Newsletter
- ★ Exclusive Mills & Boon Book Club offers
- ★ Books available before they're in the shops

Accepting these FREE books and gift places you under no obligation to buy, you may cancel at any time, even after receiving your free shipment. Simply complete your details below and return the entire page to the address below. You don't even need a stamp!

YES! Please send me 2 free Special Edition books and a surprise gift. I understand that unless you hear from me, I will receive 4 superb new titles every month for just £3.19 each, postage and packing free. I am under no obligation to purchase any books and may cancel my subscription at any time. The free books and gift will be mine to keep in any case.

E9ZEF

Ms/Mrs/Miss/Mr ....Initials........................
BLOCK CAPITALS PLEASE

Surname ....

Address..

....

....Postcode ....

Send this whole page to:
UK: FREEPOST CN81, Croydon, CR9 3WZ